The X-Rated Deal

Eugene Rookwood

Dexcel Publishing   *   Indianapolis, Indiana

The X-Rated Deal

Printed in the United States of America

An ode to good liquor, frank conversation and... the whatever that is sure to follow...

Eugene Rookwood

Chapter one

Diane Reynolds refilled her glass from a pint of vintage cognac. Her daughter won the expensive liquor in a raffle at work and they wasted little time getting started on it as soon as she brought it home. Diane was feeling real good but she frowned at her daughter Tasha who was finishing a brief phone call from her boyfriend. The call had interrupted their conversation.

"You a damn fool...lettin that man treat you like shit and you still runnin after his sorry ass!" Diane complained when Tasha hung up the phone.

"Mama you just don't know," Tasha replied.

"I don't huh? This ain't about nothing but your little hot panties."

"What?" Tasha questioned.

"Ain't nobody here but you and me okay. So we can talk," Diane assured. "I know all about hot panties cause I had them too when I was your age..."

"Still do!" Tasha responded with a smirk.

"Yeah I still do! But I know how to handle it," Diane insisted.

"You think I can't?" Tasha challenged.

"Not the way you let that man treat yo ass…naw, you don't know how to handle it! You don't know shit…but how to give it up," Diane snapped.

"I'm grown…I got to have it too you know…and I just might be in love," Tasha advised.

"Love ain't got nothing to do with this and you know it," Diane shot back. "Ya'll do it every chance you get don't cha? I know you do. I used to do it too…fucking like a bunny, staying hot and most of the time if I wasn't doing it, I was thinking about it," she confessed.

"You too?" Tasha asked in surprise.

"Hell yeah…" Diane responded, "And it wasn't until I had sex with a real man…that knew what he was doing, did I realize that all that bunny fucking wasn't about shit."

"That's why I'm hanging with Jerome," Tasha replied.

"Oh please…don't be trying to bullshit me girlfriend," Diane sighed. "I've heard ya'll doing it more than once…uh-huh. I've even seen Jerome's naked ass on top of you…fucking on my living room couch. That's okay I ain't mad about that. I done that shit too when I was your age…but the boy can't fuck honey…less than five minutes and ya'll through!" she chuckled.

"I'm way too hot for any man to stay in very long!" Tasha advised.

"Ha-ha…I'll bet Jerome told you that shit…" Diane chuckled even louder.

"Not just Jerome…any man!" Tasha insisted.

"You mean any boy!" Diane replied, still chuckling.

Tasha took a long sip from her glass. She liked the warm and cozy feeling the straight cognac delivered. "Why you so worried about my sex life anyway?" she questioned.

"Cause it has taken complete possession of you," Diane responded. "You don't do nothing else but fuck or talk about fucking. Which means you are just being frustrated by what you ain't getting? If you could get by that...then you could get on with the rest of your life," she advised.

"Oh and I guess doing some old ass man is gonna get me by that huh?"

"The right one would do you a lot of good," Diane shot back.

"Ha-ha...I'd wear an old man out before he knew what hit him," Tasha laughed.

"And just what you calling old?" Diane questioned.

"You know...any of them old men you be spending the night with. I'm sure they wear you out, but I'm young...and they can't come back quick like Jerome," Tasha giggled.

"What you mean come back quick?"

"You know...he can get back up in a few minutes," Tasha replied.

"From what I done already seen and heard, he comes fast, waits a little while, gets it back up, fucks quick and comes fast again," Diane responded.

"Yeah so?"

"Child you don't even know what it's all about," Diane insisted.

"I told you I'm too hot for any man to stay in for long...at least Jerome can come back quick!" Tasha declared defensively.

"You've never had a climax have you?"

"What do you mean?" Tasha asked.

"You know damn well what I mean. You have never had a climax with a man have you?" Diane pressed.

"Not really...but that don't mean I don't like sex! I do, I love it and a climax is no big deal," Tasha responded.

"I said those very same words too," Diane confided. "Just like you I was twenty years old and had a baby but still my panties were always on fire. I was dating a man that had everything cool I liked but he did not satisfy me and it didn't matter because I had never been satisfied. See I didn't know that not being sexually satisfied was a problem. I was divorced, had three children and was over thirty before I learned why I was so frustrated and had been most of my life," she continued.

"Let me guess...you done an old man and climaxed," Tasha put in.

"In short...yes!" Diane replied.

"What happened...I mean did rockets go off and bells ring and shit?" Tasha asked.

Diane laughed then explained. "The first time it happened the sensation was so powerful, it scared the shit out of me! I wanted to cry and laugh. I wanted him to stop and continue. My whole body was gripped by waves of powerful sensations and I can't tell you how special that feels but I can tell you how the release of that passion frees you from the frustration and self doubt that dogs you," she advised.

"I can get off by myself!" Tasha declared.

"Yeah you can and you and I know that don't mean shit!" Diane replied. "It's nothing like getting it with a man."

"So how come you got to do an old man to get off?"

"It don't have to be an old man. Just one that knows what he is doing..." Diane advised. "A man has to learn how to please a woman. It takes desire and time which is why boys don't know and a whole lot of them never learn. Most of them, like your Jerome are satisfied with getting themselves off...they don't give a damn about their women. A real man knows his greatest and most powerful pleasure comes during the passion of pleasing his woman. It really don't matter how young or old he is. What matters, is how much he knows about dealing with a woman's body and mind. Takes time to learn that shit, so I'm sure any man that could do your smart ass any good would be what you call old," she surmised.

"Mama I hate to tell you this but times have changed," Tasha laughed. "All that old fashioned shit you talking about is ancient history. I could do any of your old boyfriends and have them begging for more," she boasted.

"You don't even believe that!" Diane declared.

"What they gonna show me Jerome ain't got?" Tasha demanded. "He got a big, hard young thang...and he can slam with it...so what your old men who probably can't get it up most of the time, gonna show me?" she questioned in disgust.

"A big hard young thang is all he got and he don't know what to do with it. Trouble is you done fell in love with it cause you don't know any better...I know...I been there," Diane responded.

"So...what am I supposed to do?"

"Get with a man for a change...a real man...not a goddamn boy!" Diane replied.

"I don't want no old man," Tasha declared.

"You want to really get off for once don't you?"

"I think all that climax shit you talking is highly overrated. Jerome knows how to get down...he's cool and I like what we got," Tasha insisted.

"You ain't got shit," Diane flatly advised. "Jerome will fuck any woman that will let him."

"He will not!" Tasha snapped.

"Gimme a break Tasha!" Diane pleaded. "Jerome is a young hard dick...constantly on the prowl for pussy. He ain't looking to satisfy the pussy, oh no he's only looking to satisfy his young hard dick. He done already hit on me and your sisters...it ain't no big thing...young hormones be talking baby!" she chuckled.

"That's a lie!" Tasha shot back.

"Naw it ain't!"

"It's gotta be...you couldn't pay Jerome to do it with you!" Tasha insisted.

"You are so wrong!" Diane declared then sipped from her drink.

"No I mean it! Jerome is very particular about everything, especially his woman," Tasha assured.

"Jerome will fuck any woman," Diane repeated.

"That's a lie...and you can't prove it!" Tasha snapped.

"Don't back me into a corner and make me put the proof in your face," Diane warned. "That boy ain't the issue no way. The issue is...still...that you need a real man in your life...if not regularly at least often enough that you know the difference," she suggested.

"You just gotta put down Jerome! But your old ass boyfriends are gods. I'm sick of this shit! I really am!" Tasha wailed as she emptied her glass then poured a fresh drink. "Tell you what...if you can do Jerome, I'll do an old man...but if you can't, I don't want to hear no more about this shit...do we have a deal?" she questioned.

"You drunk!" Diane sighed.

"No I am not!" Tasha snapped. "I'm really sick of this shit...I am sick of talking about it...and I'm calling your bluff. If you can do Jerome then I will do an old man. I'll even do him four separate times okay? Four times to your one! But! If you can't do Jerome then I don't ever expect to talk about my sex life with you again! Now do we have a deal? Well..." Tasha demanded.

"You know this ain't no good idea," Diane advised.

"Do we have a deal?" Tasha questioned impatiently.

"Don't push me against the wall Tasha...cause if you push I'll do it! It's hard to look that kind of shit in the face, but you keep pushing and I'll fuck your Jerome on the living room couch while you watch. If that's what it takes to wake yo ass up, I'll damn sure do it...so don't push!" Diane snapped.

"Mama...do we have a deal or not?" Tasha demanded.

"You just gonna make me break your heart and fuck your boyfriend huh?" Diane asked.

"It's not about breaking my heart...the truth is I don't believe that antique shit you're talking," Tasha chuckled. "I don't believe you can do Jerome...I don't believe an old man can do shit for me and I don't believe you are willing to make a deal! If you can do Jerome then I don't want him. He's just a dog and I will give you credit for knowing your shit, take your advice...and sleep with an old man...four times. Now do we have a deal?" she again demanded.

"All right! Damn...enough already!" Diane snapped. "You gotta keep pushing. I'm gonna make this deal! I'm gonna fuck Jerome while you watch with tears in your eyes. I'm gonna make this deal so you can grow the fuck up! You think I'm full of shit? We'll see who's full of shit!" she fumed.

"Jerome's coming over tonight," Tasha calmly advised.

"Fine! I'll leave your sisters and the baby at Big Mama's and you can park your ass on the stairs, just above the bend where you can see but not be seen and watch Jerome fuck your mama," Diane declared.

"You tripping...Jerome ain't gonna do you!" Tasha giggled.

"If you trying to back out of the deal I understand," Diane offered.

"Oh hell naw! I ain't backing out! I can't wait to get this shit over!" Tasha insisted.

"It's settled then...you got called in to work and I'll be home alone with Jerome and we will see what happens," Diane responded.

Jerome arrived late in the evening. Diane had freshened herself and changed into a tight fitting dress. Tasha sat at the head of the stairs and watched as her mother opened the door.

"Why hello Jerome come on in," Diane gushed.

"What's up Miss D? Where Tasha?" Jerome asked.

"Tasha got called in to work tonight and the girls are at my mothers so I'm all by myself...why don't you have a drink and keep me company for awhile," Diane suggested.

"Naw...I gotta keep on moving...I got some..." Jerome began.

"Come on now Jerome! You didn't come over here planning to just stick your head in the door, did you?" Diane questioned.

"Naw...I guess not," Jerome admitted.

"What you drinking? Scotch? Gin?" Diane asked.

"Gin is cool," Jerome responded.

"Well come on over here and fix yourself a drink," Diane instructed. "I'd fix it for you but I don't know how you like it."

She turned and slowly walked across the living room, seductively grinding her ass against the form fitting fabric that tightly clung to it. In the dining room Diane bent over to get the liquor from the china cabinet knowing the young man's eyes were glued to her every move.

Jerome felt himself getting hard as he hurried into the dining room and stepped close enough to Diane that his thigh lightly touched her.

"Get a couple of glasses from the second shelf Jerome honey," Diane instructed as she pressed her ass against the young man's thigh. "Now where is that gin?" she questioned.

Though it was unnecessary to reach the glasses Jerome shifted his position. His growing hard-on now rested firmly against Diane's ass cheek.

"Here it is," Diane announced straightening up and grinding her ass against Jerome's crotch. "Oh I'm sorry Jerome honey, I didn't mean to bump into you," she chuckled.

"You got nothing to apologize for," Jerome whispered, sliding his arm around Diane's waist and pulling her ass back against his hard-on.

Diane fixed her drink while Jerome pressed his young manhood into the crack of her ass. "You better be careful honey, this ain't no little teenybopper you messing with," she warned.

"I'm down with that. I got a big ole dick and it's real hard...I know you feel it," Jerome bragged.

"Yeah I feel it all right!" Diane replied. "Now look Jerome," she continued, "if I do this and I'm not saying I will, but if I do, it ain't got nothing to do with love and there ain't no tomorrow's...do you understand that?"

Jerome was now grinding hard against Diane, squeezing her titties and kissing her neck. "Yeah...I understand. Goddamn...you pretty and soft...I'm gonna fuck the shit out of you," he promised.

"Maybe," Diane responded. "Fix your drink...then I'll see you on the couch." She placed her drink on the coffee table then hurried up the stairs. "Have you seen enough?" she whispered.

"I ain't seen nothing! All I heard is some weak talk!" Tasha shot back in a loud whisper.

Diane frowned at her daughter than quickly descended the stairs and joined Jerome on the couch. He sat next to her, put one arm around her shoulders, one hand on her knee and leaned to kiss her. Diane responded, kissing Jerome hard and deep while placing her hand on his and sliding them up her leg until his fingers rested firmly against her soft crotch. She then slid her hand up his leg finding and massaging his hard manhood. Jerome was a good kisser and his fingers quickly began to play a pleasant tune between her legs.

Diane was impressed and starting to get turned on when Jerome abruptly broke off the kiss, stood up and stepped out of his pants. He pushed Diane down, pulled off her panties then lunged on top of her and made three unsuccessful attempts before he found her opening and forced himself inside. Diane retreated from the sudden invasion but Jerome pushed harder, driving his raging hard-on in deeper. She shifted to accommodate him but was starting to get pissed off. If Jerome wasn't such a fucking wild man she could enjoy this. Jerome had a firm grip on Diane's legs and was trying his best to fuck her hard and fast when Tasha placed a gun against his temple.

"Get your slimy dick out of my mother!" she growled. "Then get your sorry ass out of my house. NOW! And don't say shit...not one fucking word now or ever, or so help me I'll blow your fucking dick off," Tasha threatened in a low chilling voice.

Jerome left the house with his pants under his arm and his dick flapping in the breeze.

*****

"Ha-ha..." Diane chuckled, "one of these days I'm gonna get some bullets for that gun...ha-ha..."

"Naw don't do that! If this gun had bullets Jerome wouldn't have no dick," Tasha snapped.

"I'm sorry baby, I didn't want to hurt you," Diane responded.

"Naw don't apologize!" Tasha insisted. "You was right! You know yo shit...okay? Jerome ain't nothing but a fucking dog! His sorry ass wasn't in the house five minutes before his dick took over. I'll give you your props. You was right about Jerome...and a deal is a deal...but the jury is still out on what an old dick can do for me!" she grumbled.

"You'll know as soon as you find one!" Diane advised.

"Aw naw...bullshit...you know that ain't right...you trying to sidestep!" Tasha declared. "The deal was that if you could do Jerome...which you did! Then I would do an old man four times. I hang with young men...you hang with old men. I provided Jerome for you...so you gotta provide an old man that can do all that shit you talked about for me!" she insisted.

"Uh-huh...I knew this wasn't no good deal," Diane complained. "Jerome was a lousy fuck and now I gotta find you a man! Shit! Well...you do need to grow up. You got the best end of this deal...matter of fact, you're gonna owe me real big when this shit is over. Now go get yo baby and your sisters and I'll start working on a man for you tomorrow," she concluded.

"Tomorrow?" Tasha questioned.

"Yeah tomorrow...if then...I gotta talk a mature grown man into breaking in a child! And that ain't gonna be easy," Diane sighed.

"Pardon me?" Tasha snapped. "I mean let's get real here...mother! You know that every old man you hooked up with would slobber all over himself at just the thought of sleeping with me!" she boasted.

"Don't fool yourself honey...grown mature men are not falling over themselves to sleep with real young women cause ya'll got a lot of baggage."

"Baggage?"

"Yeah...young children, false notions, ignorance, puppy love, crazy demands and expectations of a perfect relationship for starters. Not to mention your attitude," Diane explained.

"Attitude? What attitude?" Tasha demanded.

"Oh please...I'm gonna have to work at finding a man to deal with you!" Diane snapped. "Now go on and get yo sisters and baby and like I said...I'll let you know something tomorrow."

"I don't know what attitude you are talking about! I don't have an attitude!" Tasha insisted.

"Tasha...you're over critical, challenging and mad about every damn thing! Every time I turn around you are pissed off or unhappy about somethin or the other! Well...Miss hot-in-the-pants...the right man will take care of a lot of that shit. You're right! A deal is a deal and I'm damn sure gonna hook you up. Now go!" Diane demanded.

"The deal was for four times...I'd like to get that over with as soon as possible!"

"You go pick up them children and let me worry about the first time," Diane responded.

"All right, all right...I'm going...God! I could kick Jerome's ass again and again!" Tasha fumed.

Diane was not a happy woman. Her concern for her daughter had exploded into a showdown that now required she share a lover with her. It was not a comfortable thought. Diane didn't share her men and knew that in many ways Tasha was a young version of her. A young version her older lovers might find irresistible. She had three lovers and didn't want to lose any one of them. Yet, because she had actually allowed her daughter's boyfriend to penetrate her, she was over a barrel and would have to trust one of her men to make love to Tasha and still prefer her when it was over.

Reluctantly and with great anguish Diane chose Elliott Johnson to become Tasha's lover and teacher. Elliott was a bachelor in his mid-forties, once divorced with no children who lived alone. He was intelligent, physically fit, an excellent lover and would most likely keep the experience in perspective. Her relationship with Elliott was great but it was also casual and infrequent, so Diane had the least to lose if she lost him to Tasha. After a few hours of trying and failing to think of a way out of the deal she wished she had not made, Diane dialed Elliott's number with hopeful resignation.

"Hello?" Elliott spoke into the phone.

"Hi...hi ya doing?" Diane replied.

"Hey now...what's up with you?" Elliott questioned.

"Oh...nothing...just thought I would see if you are going to be busy this weekend?"

"Need to get away huh?"

"Well yes and no. I need you to do something for me and this is something you are going to like!" Diane promised.

"No shit! What is it?"

"I don't want to talk about it on the phone, I'll just wait till I come over and tell you about it in person," Diane responded.

"Hum...some freaky shit huh? Freaky deaky!" Elliott teased.

"Stop that!" Diane chided. "I said I don't want to talk about it on the phone!"

"Ha-ha...okay...so when you want to come over?" "Will you be home tomorrow evening?" Diane asked.

"I will be if yo freaky ass is coming over!" Elliott replied.

"Ha-ha..." Diane chuckled, "uh-huh...well I ain't promising...but I'm gonna try. If I can't make it I'll let you know okay?" she asked.

"Uh-huh...don't be fucking with my head now girl...either one of em,"

"Ha-ha...I got some head for your head!" Diane offered.

"I know you do...and I sho need it too!"

"Ha-ha...you silly..." Diane giggled, "ha-ha...I'll see you tomorrow."

"Okay then...see you tomorrow," Elliott agreed.

"Okay bye," Diane purred.

"Bye."

A porno movie played on the television as Elliott relaxed on his couch. Diane sat atop a large pillow on the floor, comfortably nestled between his naked legs playing with his dick. She massaged the head of it with her tongue then sucked up and down making it wet and nasty, just the way Elliott loved it. Little did he know Diane was on a mission to make sure that he knew just how good she really was. She licked his balls and the shaft underneath then shifted to her knees and began sucking his dick rapidly up and down. Elliott stroked her hair and pumped into her hot mouth while grinding his hips and moaning which greatly pleased Diane.

After a few minutes she stood up and straddled Elliott then lowered her knees to the couch guiding her pussy to his hard-on. Elliott reached out and diverted his dick to Diane's clit then lightly rubbed it back and forth. Delighted, Diane lowered herself even more. Sliding and grinding her pussy on Elliott's delicious male meat. She humped up and down until Elliott stopped her then massaged her clit with just the head of his dick and their wet sticky juices. Diane felt that certain tingle began to surge through her body. Using her hands she spread herself as wide as she could completely exposing her sensitive and very swollen clit. Elliott grabbed her ass and maintained a gentle but firm rhythm, riding her clit slowly against the head of his hard-on until her body convulsed and trembled with the power of impending climax. Elliott's throbbing hard-on slid deep inside Diane just as her orgasm peaked, causing her to scream then gyrate and hump in impossible patterns. For several minutes Diane bounced up and down, riding Elliott and tripping on the feelings her body was serving up. Elliott smiled and lightly stroked her thighs. It was a great fuck and he was enjoying it.

Diane was literally on fire as her entire body tingled and quivered. She loved dick...especially Elliott's good dick. She had wanted Elliott to know just how good she really was and held nothing back, but found herself overwhelmed by a heady rush of lust and passion that gripped and excited her. Diane pressed her tits against Elliott's chest, buried her face in his neck and clawed at his hair as tingling sensations flooded over her. Her ass trembled then shook but Elliott held her tight and pumped deep in and out. Diane again cried out then covered his mouth with hers, sparking a long slow session of kissing and deep grinding.

Finally Diane leaned back and squeezed Elliott's still hard dick, it felt good buried inside her. She looked into his eyes and smiled. "I like this shit," she purred.

"Yeah...shit is good ain't it?" Elliott agreed.

"Better than good!" Diane exclaimed.

Elliott began sucking Diane's nipples while she closed her eyes and gave herself to the feeling. Slowly siding up and down Elliott's hard-on while he made her nipples hard, teasing their sensitivity. Again passion rose and both of them were soon deep into the throes of another wave of sensations that rocked their collective world.

"Fuck me baby! Aw yeah...take me! Take me!" Diane cried out.

"Work it girl! Suck this dick with that pussy!" Elliott demanded. "Uh huh...uh-huh just like that. Fuck that dick girl...sheeit! Do it baby...fuck me Diane...shit! Now fuck me! Fuck me freak! Whew...shit...that's it...work that pussy Diane...umm...umm..." Elliott went back to work on Diane's nipples while she violently fucked him until both of them exploded in a powerful climax.

A few moments later Diane whispered into Elliott's ear. "You know you good don't you?"

"Uh-huh...I know I'm good when I'm inside you!" he responded.

"You good! The best!" Diane insisted. "That's why I want you to do something for me."

"Uh-huh...I'm listening."

"I want you to do Tasha," Diane advised.

"What?" Elliott questioned in confused surprise.

"Look it's a long story okay...she's frustrated cause she's rabbit fucking dumb young boys. She really needs to learn how to make love and get off," Diane explained.

"Oh I got to teach her how to fuck too...huh?" Elliott responded.

"You are the best!" Diane declared. "You taught me baby...that's why I want you to teach her."

"Yeah...right!" Elliott replied with a dry chuckle.

"I mean it! I'm serious! I want you to do Tasha!" Diane insisted.

"Does Tasha happen to know about this?"

"Of course," Diane responded. "She ain't real thrilled about it but we made a bet and she lost...now she got to sleep with who I say and I want her to take lessons from you."

"You asking a lot from one fuck!" Elliott complained.

"Not one...four fucks darling!" Diane countered.

"What...? Four?" Elliott questioned again in surprise.

"That's right! The bet was for her to fuck you four times," Diane explained.

"Four different nights or four times in one night?" Elliott asked still unsure about the whole thing.

"Four different nights okay? Now are you gonna do it? Please?"

"I don't know about this," Elliott hedged. "What were you two betting on?"

"Girl stuff," Diane answered, "but that doesn't matter because she lost. She's a hot young thing in need and she's yours for four nights if you say okay. Please say okay Elliott."

"Is she on the pill?"

"Of course she is!"

"You're sure, real sure?"

"She is on the pill, now please say you will do it," Diane pleaded.

"Yeah...all right," Elliott reluctantly agreed, "but I hope her head is in the right place...young pussy usually comes with a damn attitude," he sighed.

"I can't believe I'm actually asking you to do this either but I know it's what she really needs," Diane responded. "Just put this sweet meat on her...show her what it's all about...then cut her loose. That's all I ask, okay?"

"Hum...okay...I'll deal with her next week but right now I'm not finished with you!" Elliott responded then stood up and led Diane to his bed.

After she sucked him hard, he positioned her on her back at the edge of the bed so he could stand. With her legs against his shoulders, he slid all the way into her and began fucking in long, delicious wet strokes. Diane arched her back and grabbed the sheets as they fucked hard, grinding and bumping against each other until yet another orgasm seized Diane. Elliott didn't let up; he continued to pump his hard-on into her for several moments before turning a delighted Diane onto her stomach. He climbed on top of her, slid his manhood down the crack of her ass, between her pussy lips then on to briefly massage her swollen clit before pushing deep inside. The feel of her hot wet pussy on his dick and her soft freaky ass pushing against his crotch was the ultimate for Elliott. He rose up and pumped hard into Diane, his hips and crotch slamming against her ass cheeks until that groundswell of undeniable sensation swept through his body, stretching his dick to its limit then exploding in a glorious rush. Elliott collapsed then floated in ecstasy as Diane's soft wet pussy eagerly milked and massaged his still throbbing dick.

Elliott and Diane knew what they were doing and they were good together, very good. They sexually teased then satisfied the deep animalistic passion within one another. Elliott truly enjoyed having sex with Diane, she was good and fun in bed. He thought about Tasha and hoped she would be even better. In fact the more he thought about it, the more he looked forward to fucking Diane's daughter.

Chapter two

*T*he *following Friday* Tasha watched her mother's car disappear down the street then stepped through the door into Elliott's living room.

"Come on in sweetheart...make yourself comfortable. You want a drink?" Elliott welcomed with a smile.

"Yeah...rum and make it strong!" Tasha responded. "You got any rap music?"

"Naw...I got some good stuff though," Elliott replied. He poured two ounces of cola over an ounce of rum then added a few cubes of ice. "Here you go."

"You call this shit a drink?" Tasha snapped. "I can't even taste the liquor!" She poured close to a double shot of rum on top of her drink then drank it all, stopping only twice before she emptied the glass.

"Shit! Now that's what I call thirsty," Elliott grinned. "You want another baby-girl? Go ahead help yourself," he offered.

"No I don't want another..." Tasha snarled, "and I didn't come here to socialize! I came here to fuck! So let's do it and get it over with," she demanded.

"Would you be offended it we tried to enjoy it a little?" Elliott questioned. "How about I put on some music?"

"Damn the music! Just hurry up and fuck me so I can get the hell out of here!" Tasha insisted.

"Well if you hate the thought all that bad why in the hell did you come over here in the first place?" Elliott questioned with growing frustration.

"Why you care? All you gotta do is fuck me!" Tasha shot back, removing her clothes as she talked.

Elliott ignored her, found a Marvin Gaye tape and put it into his stereo.

"Ain't you got nothing better than that old fashioned shit?" Tasha complained. "Never mind let's just fuck."

"You ever hear of foreplay?" Elliott asked.

"No! But I've heard about old ass men that can't get it up," Tasha responded as she removed the last of her clothes and stood completely naked. Her tight young body was stacked with large firm tits, a narrow waist and a very round ass.

Elliott was impressed and despite her antagonism he felt his manhood starting to rise. "I don't do wham bam thank you ma'am...but in your case I'll try," he offered.

"Oh thank you so fucking much! Now can we get this shit over with!" Tasha snapped.

"All right if that's the way you want it...come on," Elliott replied then led Tasha to his bed, silently admiring her body as he slowly began to undress.

"Will you come on! Goddamn...I do plan to have some real fun tonight...so hurry the fuck up!" Tasha demanded.

Elliott was becoming agitated. Iin spite of her body Tasha's mouth was turning him off. He stood naked for a moment and stroked himself.

"I didn't come here to watch you play with yourself!" Tasha hissed. "Come on!"

Elliott shook his head and climbed on top of Tasha. He attempted to raise her legs but she insisted on keeping them flat on the bed, so Elliott struggled to get the head of his dick into her. She was barely moist so he backed out, rolled onto his side wet his fingers and began using them on her, hoping she would loosen up and let her juices flow.

"I can finger fuck myself...I didn't come here for that!" Tasha snapped.

"Oh shut the fuck up! I'm tired of yo shit!" Elliott growled. He grabbed a tube of K-Y jelly, greased his dick and rolled back on top of Tasha. He pushed into her and tried to pump in and out but Tasha lay perfectly still and stared at the ceiling. She resisted any movement or repositioning of herself and Elliott was quickly becoming frustrated and losing interest. "Damn can't you raise your legs or move your ass a little," he asked.

"You supposed to be fucking me!" Tasha coldly advised.

"It takes two to tango you know," Elliott responded.

"Naw the truth is you supposed to be some kind of fucking God that is going to rock my world and you ain't done shit!" Tasha declared.

"Can't nobody do shit for you if you don't cooperate," Elliott explained.

"Admit it! This pussy is too much for you ain't it?" Tasha demanded.

"What! Too much?" Elliott questioned defensively. He raised his upper body and tried hard to fuck Tasha but it wasn't good. She stared at the ceiling and didn't move. Their position was bad and after a few frustrating moments Elliott began to lose his hard-on. He rolled off Tasha, lay on his back and stared at the ceiling.

"I knew you couldn't keep it up!" Tasha announced sarcastically. "Is that it?"

"Yeah that's it! Fuck it!" Elliott growled.

"Pardon me?" Tasha questioned with indignation. "It's not my fault you can't keep it up. And it's not my fault you can't hang with this pussy!" she sharply criticized.

"Long as you just gonna lay there like a mummy can't nobody do much of nothing with yo ass," Elliott snapped.

"What you want me to do?" Tasha asked.

"Cooperate damnit! Let me move you around, raise your legs, get in there right!" Elliott suggested.

"Naw here the pussy is and you just can't hang with it. You can't even cum. All you can do is beat your own meat, like you doing now," Tasha responded.

Elliott was stroking himself back to hard and plenty sick of Tasha. He stepped off the bed, grabbed her legs, yanked her to the edge of the bed, held her legs up and apart with his forearms pushed his dick into her and again attempted to pump in and out. He tried hard but the weight of her legs made fucking difficult. Tasha remained impassive, staring at the ceiling and resisting any signal-of-pleasure her body hinted at. Finally Elliott pushed into her and leaned forward to rest.

"Is that it? Did you cum?" Tasha demanded.

"No I didn't cum, I'm just trying to change position a little," Elliott replied.

"You mean your ass is wore out! Old…tired and worn out!" Tasha taunted. "And you supposed to do something for me…sheeit…first you can't keep it up…then you can't even cum…sheeit!" she snorted.

"Yeah…you right that's it!" Elliott snapped. He pulled out, dropped Tasha legs then washed up and put his clothes on. "Thought you was in such a fucking hurry to get out of here?" he questioned. "Come on get your shit on…I'll take you home."

"You throwing me out?" Tasha questioned.

"Yeah something like that!" Elliott replied.

Tasha washed and slowly put her clothes on in silence, then made a weak offer. "Look I know I brought a little attitude with me this time, but next time I'm gonna bring a joint and maybe party a little first," she suggested.

"Fuck a next time!" Elliott snapped. "You ready?"

"Don't be like that! I'm just really uptight today…okay?" Tasha pleaded.

"Yeah maybe…you ready to go?" Elliott replied.

"Yeah I'm ready…hey look I meant what I said about bringing a joint, it loosens me up and makes me all horny and shit…you'll see," Tasha promised.

"Yeah…right," Elliott responded.

They drove in silence until Elliott stopped his car in front of Tasha's house.

"Can I come over tomorrow?" she asked.

"No!"

"How about Sunday?"

"No!

"You are going to let me come back aren't you?" Tasha pleaded.

"I'll think about it!" Elliott responded.

"Come on now...I said I was sorry about today...damn!" Tasha whined.

"And I said I'll think about it!"

"Okay...I'll call you," Tasha offered.

"Fine," Elliott agreed with little interest.

"Bye-bye and don't be mad at me okay?" Tasha responded as she stepped from the car.

"Yeah...Bye!" Elliott grunted.

Diane was stunned and could not believe what she was hearing. She was damn disappointed with Tasha and wanted to call the deal off but Tasha was adamant about seeing it through.

Tasha wasn't happy with herself. First Elliott made her feel guilty about her behavior now her mother made it worse. She had wanted to prove that Elliott was not a better lover than Jerome and had purposely given Elliott a hard time. Tasha knew that wasn't fair, but she was still angry with Jerome and her mother. How dare he put his thing into her...and how dare she actually let him. She went to Elliott's house determined not to come home gushing about how great he was. Now she felt lousy, none of this was going like she had hoped. Despite their rocky beginning Tasha was impressed with Elliott and assured her mother that her behavior would improve. She called Elliott but he hung up on her. Two days later Tasha again called

Elliott, he was impatient and promised nothing, agreeing only to talk to her again. Finally after two more phone conversations Elliott relented and agreed to share his bed with her one more time.

Tasha arrived at Elliott's house smiling, high on weed and carrying a handful of rap tapes, which Elliott refused to play, putting on soft music instead. After fixing drinks they settled onto the sofa. Tasha attempted to apologize but Elliott insisted that bygones were bygones. He was more interested in their getting to know each other. Their conversation was pleasant and punctuated with laughter and light kisses that grew more and more passionate. Soon they were completely undressed and tasting more of each others flesh.

Tasha was losing herself to Elliott's advances until he asked if she wanted to suck him. "What?" she snapped. "Hell naw! I ain't no hoe! I don't do that nasty shit! You think I'm a hoe don't you?"

"No I don't think that. You wouldn't be here if I thought that," Elliott assured.

"Yes you do!" Tasha insisted. "Why else would you ask me to do some nasty shit like that!"

"It's not nasty...it's all a part of lovemaking," Elliott explained.

"Bullshit! It is too...you old bastard! You think I'm a dumb young hoe you can fuck over!" Tasha fumed. "Well I'm not! I ain't putting no man's dick in my mouth...asshole!"

"Tasha...damn," Elliott responded. "I thought maybe you were a little more mature than you are...okay...so just forget about it. It's no big thing, some women enjoy it others don't...but it's not important enough to ruin a nice evening," he suggested.

"I can't believe your punk ass tried to make me do some nasty shit like that," Tasha snorted.

"Now look...I ain't got to be all them foul names," Elliott advised with slight irritation creeping into his voice.

"You lucky I ain't kicked yo ass!" Tasha threatened.

"What!" Elliott snapped.

"You heard me punk!" Tasha challenged.

"I hope you try it...bitch!" Elliott shot back.

"What the fuck you call me!" Tasha demanded.

"You ain't deaf...and you ain't the only one who can call people out of their name," Elliott replied.

"Look! Nobody calls me that. I been trying to be nice to your old ass, but if you don't take that back I'm gonna kick your butt and I mean it!" Tasha insisted.

"Ha-ha-ha..." Elliott chuckled.

"Oh that's funny huh?" Tasha growled, then swung but Elliott caught her arm.

"Don't even try it silly girl," Elliott chuckled just as Tasha broke from his grip and began slapping at him with both hands. After struggling for a few moments Elliott got control of Tasha, wrestled her down and covered her mouth with a passionate kiss that grew hot, sloppy and intense. He then picked her up and carried her to his bed.

When he laid Tasha on her back she again started swinging her arms trying to slap him, so he grabbed her arms and again covered her mouth with his. Tasha responded, sucking his tongue, grinding her hips then raising her legs. He released her arms and she grabbed his shoulders, whimpering as his hard-on slid into her. Elliott was amazed, Tasha was incredibly hot and wet.

He pushed further into her feeling an exciting wave of sensual pleasure sweep over his body. For several moments the two of them held tight to each other, locked in a wet passionate kiss, while Elliott slowly stroked in and out. Tasha caught his rhythm and began raising her hips to meet his thrust as gradually the speed and passion intensified. Elliott was delighted and just about to really get down to some serious lovemaking when Tasha bit hard into his lip and dug her fingernails into his back.

"Ouch! Goddamnit! You crazy bitch?" Elliott wailed.

Tasha bolted, knocking Elliott off balance but he grabbed her and rolled onto his back with her on top of him. She pushed away pinning his shoulders to the bed, but he held on to her ass and worked her hips until his dick was again deep inside her. It felt good and her struggling made it even better. After a few moments Tasha quit struggling and leaned back, bouncing slightly in rhythm with Elliott's thrusting dick, then suddenly she slapped him hard across his face. Elliott threw Tasha off of him, put one foot against her thigh and kicked her out of his bed. But, much to his surprise, she sprang from the floor and tackled him before he could get off the bed.

"Who you kicking out of bed? Apologize damnit!" she demanded. "And apologize for calling me that name...twice!"

"Go back to hell...she devil!" Elliott snapped.

"You better apologize!" Tasha threatened.

Elliott wrestled free and got control of Tasha. "What's up with you? You into rough sex...or what?" he questioned.

Tasha struggled. "Let me go!" she demanded.

"You gonna be cool?" Elliott asked.

"You gonna apologize?" Tasha shot back.

"Hell naw! You can't take it...don't be trying to dish it out," Elliott responded.

"Then I'm gonna kick yo ass!" Tasha insisted.

"Ha-ha-ha..." Elliott chuckled again.

"Don't be laughing at me! Old punk mutherfucker!" Tasha snapped. "Yeah you can hold me down and slam a little...for a minute, but you can't do shit else! You can't even cum! And you supposed to be so bad!" she taunted.

"I can't huh?" Elliott questioned.

"I ain't seen none...boy!" Tasha replied.

"For your information, climax is as much mental as it is physical so mostly I cum when I want to," Elliott advised with a smile.

"Bullshit! You can't cum! You can't handle this pussy and you ain't man enough to apologize for insulting me...now let me go so I can kick your ass!" Tasha demanded.

"You tripping..." Elliott chuckled.

"Naw you the one tripping! You lucky to even be in bed with me...your old sorry ass can't fuck and can't cum!" Tasha snapped.

"That done it!" Elliott declared then quickly stepped off the bed and yanked Tasha to the edge, pinning her legs against her shoulders. Amazed that he was rock hard, he pushed into her and was even more amazed to find her even hotter and wetter than before. Elliott could not deny that on this night Tasha felt absolutely sensational to him. He pushed his entire dick into her, withdrew and pushed all of it in again. Soon he was fucking her hard with smooth precision. She began to whimper while he was deep grinding into her and he knew she would climax if he kept it up. He also knew he would cum if he went back to long stroking her, so he went back to long stroking. A few more long wet strokes produced that incredible feeling. Tasha was good, really good. Elliott dearly wanted to stay in her but pulled out and came on her titties and stomach.

"Ooohh! You nasty old mutherfucker! You didn't have to do that!"

"You wanted cum...you got cum," Elliott replied.

"But you didn't have to cum all over me! That's just fucking nasty! Goddamnit! Ewe...shit!" Tasha wailed then hurried to the shower.

Elliott relaxed; he was spent and had dozed off by the time Tasha finished her shower. She dressed before hitting him hard across his ass with her shoe.

"What the fuck!" Elliott questioned in angry confusion.

"I ain't through with yo ass!" Tasha declared. "You still owe me an apology...punk!"

"Goddamnit you crazy bit...knuckle head! I done told you, don't be calling me foul names and I won't call you any!" Elliott snapped.

"It's too late for that shit...you done insulted me...now apologize mutherfucker! I mean it!" Tasha demanded.

"You hit me again and I'm gonna take you out! Now give it a rest damnit!" Elliott growled.

"I'm ready to go!" Tasha announced.

"Yes you are!" Elliott agreed then quickly dressed and again drove Tasha home in silence.

When they arrived at her house, Tasha stepped from the car, held the door open and once again demanded an apology.

"No!" Elliott replied.

"Punk!" Tasha snapped.

"Bitch!" Elliott responded.

She slammed the door and Elliott sped away.

Tasha watched Elliott's car brake then turn the corner and disappear. She did not feel like facing Diane so she crossed the street and went to Louise's house.

Louise Wilson was a long time family friend and infrequent babysitter. She was thirty-seven years old but Tasha considered Louise more of a big sister than baby-sitter or just friend. She brought Louise up to date on her experiences with Elliott and the reason for them. When she finished her story, Louise was shaking her head. "Girl! I don't believe you!" Louise gasped.

"What?" Tasha questioned.

"In the first place I can't believe you'd go and challenge yo mama like that," Louise explained. "You oughta know Diane ain't gonna make no bet less she knows she gonna win. And why you dogging that poor man?" she asked.

"I told you he wanted to put his thang in my mouth!" Tasha pouted.

"So!" Louise responded.

"So? That shit is nasty!" Tasha declared.

"Who told you that?" Louise questioned.

"I learned that shit in high school...in health class!"

"Woman teacher?" Louise asked.

"Yeah why?"

"Bet she ain't got no man," Louise chuckled.

"That ain't got nothing to do with it! That shit is nasty...only hoes do shit like that! Bet you don't do it!" Tasha challenged.

"That's another bet you would lose," Louise responded with a grin.

"What? You do that shit?" Tasha question in surprise.

"Tasha...damn! It's all a part of lovemaking," Louise declared. "There's more to your body and more to sex than just your thang."

"You sound like Elliott!"

"Well maybe the man was trying to teach yo ass something!"

"I can't believe you are saying this!" Tasha declared.

"Yes you can, you done already said he took you up a notch tonight," Louise shot back.

"I didn't say that!"

"Honey it's in your voice! Admit it...the man shook yo booty a little tonight...didn't he?" Louise questioned with a smile.

"A little...maybe," Tasha admitted, "but he called me that B word!"

Louise fixed drinks then sat back down. "Tasha...honey..." she began, "there comes a time in a female's life when she has the chance to cross that bridge from girl to woman. She can't cross that bridge alone...she needs a man. Not just any man either. Boys can't even get her started right and some men can only get her part of the way. The wrong man can get her stranded, but the right man can get her all the way across. And it sounds to me like Diane hooked you up with the right man. So why don't you chill out honey?

The man's trying to be nice to you...and you're the only one with anything to gain!" Louise advised.

"Pardon me!" Tasha snapped. "An old man gets to sleep with my young, high yella ass four times and I'm the only one with anything to gain?"

"That's what I said!" Louise shot back. "There is plenty young yella ass around, yours ain't nothing special. You said the man has his own house didn't you? He could have a house full of live-in young yella asses if he wanted it! Believe me honey...you're the only one with anything to gain here," she declared.

"I don't believe this shit!" Tasha barked. "I'm just supposed to kiss his butt huh?"

"You supposed to relax and let the man teach you something," Louise instructed. "It ain't that big a sacrifice. Everybody that really knows how to enjoy sex had to be taught. The sooner you learn, the longer you have to really enjoy what you got. And shame on them that don't ever learn!"

"And I guess I'm supposed to let him put his thang in my mouth too!" Tasha questioned with a sneer.

"Yes...and when he puts his mouth on yours, you'll understand why!" Louise explained.

"Aw naw...no way...you just talking shit ain't cha?" Tasha chided.

"What you oughta do is offer to fix dinner for him to make up then let him take it from there," Louise advised.

"What? Naw...I think yo ass been cooped up in this house too long and you getting desperate," Tasha giggled.

"Tasha...go home!" Louise demanded. "Go on, we done talked enough for one day."

Diane was outraged. The words exchanged between her and Tasha was more than just a little heated. Diane again wanted to cancel the deal but Tasha insisted on seeing it through, so Diane promised Tasha that if she mistreated Elliott again, she would fuck Jerome ten times for every one time she tormented Elliott. That could be up to forty times and somehow Tasha knew Diane meant it and would make sure she saw or knew about all forty times. Tasha no longer wanted anything to do with Jerome, she didn't want to see him and she certainly did not want to see him fuck Diane again.

Inside Tasha was a mess; her firm held values and beliefs were being attacked from all sides. Her position was quickly losing ground but her ego was fighting hard. Admitting ignorance or being wrong was a hard pill for Tasha to swallow, so a couple of days later she had sex with a young friend. It was a quick, half-dry fuck that lacked a lot to be desired.

The next day she had sex again with the same friend. More time but the same result. He came but she got nothing. Finally Tasha had to admit that Elliott had aroused some deep sexual feelings in her. She liked them and wanted more. She had sex with another boy hoping that he would arouse her, but it too was a disaster. He was clumsy, rough and came way to fast. Tasha was truly pissed, a general without any troops. Her staunch position had crumbled, leaving neither defense nor shelter and she had to admit to herself that now she actually needed Elliott. She needed more of the feelings he aroused within her that second time with him. She needed him and she was afraid of that feeling. Afraid to admit that she not only needed him...she wanted him, she was hot for him. Hot for Elliott Johnson, an old man that didn't seem quite so old anymore. She was afraid of losing control...afraid of falling in love and afraid of being rejected in the end.

Tasha sulked for three more days then called Elliott. At first he was reluctant and didn't want to talk but her pleading and the tone of her voice convinced Elliott to stay on the phone. Their conversation grew warm, intense then erotic, lasting for almost an hour. When Tasha hung up the phone her panties were wet. She vigorously shook her head, grinned broadly into her mirror then stuck out her tits and strutted around her bedroom. Not only had she successfully arranged the third date with Elliott...she had been invited to dinner. A dinner they would both cook in his kitchen.

Chapter three

Diane *was greatly relieved* when she heard of Tasha's dinner invitation but anxiety began to gnaw at her. Elliott had tolerated Tasha's attitude and bad behavior twice without going off on either of them...and now a dinner invitation? Diane was keenly aware of the subtle changes in Tasha's behavior and while it was something she knew her daughter needed, she feared Tasha would become smitten and Elliott would be forced to choose between them.

Louise on the other hand was delighted to hear about the dinner invitation. She advised Tasha to take an overnight bag, leave any attitude at home and be as nice to the man as he is being to you. "Relax and enjoy yourself honey," she instructed. "There is nothing to prove and everything to gain."

It was the advice of Louise that Tasha reflected on that following Friday evening as she scurried about Elliott's kitchen preparing dinner. Elliott set an elegant table, fixed drinks, rolled a joint then popped in and out of the kitchen. He opened something or chopped something, nuzzled and complimented Tasha then busied himself in other parts of the house until dinner was ready. Their candlelit dinner was complete with good music, a floral setting and vintage wine. Tasha blushed hard all during dinner as Elliott sincerely complimented her cooking. Never had she experienced so elegant a dinner and she was deeply impressed. Elliott was pleased Tasha was growing up before his very eyes and already was one damn good cook.

After dinner, Elliott led Tasha to the living room. He poured brandy, lit a joint and the two of them snuggled close on the sofa. They were feeling no pain when the increasing tempo of the music got to Elliott and he pulled Tasha to her feet, spun her around then began dancing. They danced for several minutes until Elliott again spun Tasha around and let her go, encouraging her to dance by herself while he poured more brandy. She danced shyly and slowly until Elliott again joined her, unbuttoning her clothes and whispering sweet nothings into her ear.

The music slowed and Tasha began to shed her clothes while Elliott deeply admired and lavishly complimented her impressive body. He slipped out of his clothes and for a few moments watched Tasha sensuously grind to the music. He knew she was really trying hard to please him and in that process she was getting swept up in the raw sensuality of the evening and that thrilled him. Elliott pulled Tasha into his arms and began to slow dance. Desire and passion flowed as they gradually became locked in a tight embrace. Slowly gyrating their naked bodies against each other while their hungry lips lightly touched repeatedly in a hot tantalizing tease; as all their previous conflicts melted into unbridled sexual heat. Overwhelmed Tasha began to sink to the floor and she took Elliott with her. Lying on the carpet he shifted slightly and slid his throbbing hard-on into her. She whimpered with delight for several minutes as they kissed, made love and rode a mutually thrilling wave of lust and passion.

It was almost too good, so Elliott picked up Tasha and carried her to his bed. He laid her on her back, climbed on top, slid into her then lowered his upper body into her waiting arms. She wrapped her legs around him and they settled into a hot deep grinding rhythm that soon had Tasha loudly whimpering and clawing at Elliott's head and back. As Elliott moved deep within Tasha, the little girl left and the woman arrived, taking her into new and unfamiliar territory. Long fingers of pure delight slowly began to sliver throughout her body. She quivered then cried out when those tingling fingers centered on her most sensitive flesh causing involuntary contractions and spasms. Elliott continued to stroke deep within her, causing her contractions and tingling flesh to explode in a powerful shuddering climax.

Tasha's first real orgasm and it caused her whole body to shake while she grabbed and held tight to Elliott's ass trying to pull him even deeper into her. She screamed in obvious delight then cried out, "Ooooh! Ooooh! Elliott! Elliott! Ooooh! Baby! Oooooh!"

The passion in her voice and the pure delight of her hot young body was simply too much for Elliott. He held tightly to Tasha and rode deep into her. His dick was in heaven but it was the look in her eyes that caused his cum to quickly build then explode in one exquisite uncontrollable moment.

Exhausted and thrilled, each was impressed and feeling really good about the other. They snuggled and relaxed for close to an hour before Elliott left the bed. A few moments later he returned, collected Tasha, led her to a waiting bubble bath then left her alone. Tasha settled into the hot soapy water feeling on top of the world. She completely relaxed as a deep sense of satisfaction and peace settled within her. Several minutes later Elliott returned, opened the drain, turned on the shower and joined her. Water splashed and steam rose as the two of them lost themselves to hot, wet, soapy, sex play. Finally they emerged from the shower, quickly toweled each other dry then hurried back to bed.

Tasha was completely overwhelmed! Never had she experienced such intense passion. Elliott's slightest touch made her entire body quiver and tingle. She lay back and closed her eyes delighted to hear Elliott tell her she was beautiful, sexy and smart. He kissed her ears and neck, then spent several minutes squeezing, licking and sucking her titties. Intoxicated, Tasha floated as Elliott's kiss drifted to her stomach. She jerked however when his tongue touched her inner thigh. The intensity of that feeling was incredible. Suddenly she was on fire. Her heart beat fast while tingling sensations raced through her thighs and stomach then radiated to the center of her being. Elliott was in no hurry. He kissed up and down her inner thighs for several long moments...driving Tasha absolutely insane. When his tongue began circling around her pussy while his hands massaged her nipples it caused Tasha to cry out and thrash about. Excited, she flashed back on her conversation with Louise then gladly surrendered. Never had she wanted anyone as badly as she now wanted this man. When his tongue lightly touched her most sensitive flesh the rush that flooded over Tasha nearly caused her to lose consciousness.

"No...no...ooooh no. No!" she moaned as his educated tongue flicked back and forth across her clit. The thrills had only began for Tasha as Elliott's tongue danced, his lips sucked her in and he got down to serious business. Knowing this was her first time for oral sex, Elliott truly enjoyed taking Tasha on this trip from which she would never return.

*****

Meanwhile on that same Friday evening Diane was finishing her chores and really looking forward to having the entire weekend to herself. She had pleasantly surprised Big Mama by leaving Tasha's baby with her. Her two younger daughters were spending the weekend with their father and she had dropped Tasha off at Elliott's house. Diane had been to the bank, the dry cleaners, liquor store and was coming out of the grocery when she ran smack into Jerome.

"Hey Miss D!" he called out." Wazzup...huh?"

"Why hello Jerome," Diane replied.

"Dat was cold what ya'll done to me...you know that don't you!" Jerome demanded.

"You right baby that was cold," Diane confessed. "I'm sorry Jerome honey...I really am!" she apologized.

"It wasn't you Miss D!" Jerome explained. "It was Tasha's crazy ass! I like Tasha and everything Miss D, but her temper be too hot for me to deal with," he declared.

"You just have to give her time Jerome," Diane advised.

"Yeah...I'll give her from now on...cause I don't play that shit Miss D!" Jerome fumed. "She put a big fucking gun to my head...made me run outside naked! I heard ya'll laughing at my ass when I was hiding in the bushes putting my pants on. That's some cold shit!" he complained.

"Aw honey...we didn't mean to hurt you," Diane consoled.

"You didn't...but Tasha did! And that's why we through!" Jerome declared.

"Come on now Jerome!" Diane scolded.

"Naw...I mean it. Me and Tasha through!" Jerome insisted. "Anyhow you and me got some unfinished business don't we Miss D?" he questioned with a growing smile.

"I don't know about that Jerome!" Diane weakly replied.

"Come on now Miss D it's the least you can do for me after what happened," Jerome pleaded. "And I really dig you...my shit hard already," he grinned.

Diane thought about their previous encounter and just how big Jerome's young manhood really was. She looked deep into his eyes and felt guilty for using him. She also felt sorry for his lost wandering state of being. Just like Tasha, Jerome badly needed lessons in lovemaking. "Jerome...help me get these groceries to my car," she instructed, "then you can help me get them in the house."

Diane first made two large drinks then put away the groceries. She sipped her drink then bent over and or stretched several times while putting items into the refrigerator and cabinets. She took her time because she knew Jerome's eyes were glued to her every move. Except for their brief interlude on her couch, Diane had never had sex with a man so much younger. She attempted light conversation but her passion was being inflamed by Jerome's overt lust. The big bulge in his pants proved this muscular young stud was totally hot for her and that fact deeply pleased and further aroused Diane. He really wasn't Tasha's boyfriend any longer but he was forbidden fruit and that only added to Diane's growing excitement. On this evening he was hers to ravish and enjoy. So after completing her chores in the kitchen she took the young man by the hand and led him to her bedroom.

After placing their drinks on the nightstand, Diane apologized again for using Jerome then took him into her arms and passionately kissed him. Because he was half her age Diane knew she was the one in charge and that created a new found feeling of sexual power within her. She walked across the room and leaned against the dresser then instructed her young stud to undress, make himself comfortable on the bed and finish his drink. It was a feast for Diane's eyes when Jerome stood completely naked, revealing a tight, dark brown, muscular young body with a big full-blown hard on. He sat down on the bed and gulped his drink as raw sexual lust coursed through Diane's body.

To Jerome's delight Diane slowly began to undress, teasing and taunting him until she too was completely naked. She drained her glass, licked her lips then informed Jerome that even though he had a really big dick, he did not know how to fuck and had no idea of how to please a woman or even increase his own pleasure. She walked across the room and stood close to the bed looking down at Jerome then informed him that tonight she was going to teach him how to use that big dick and how to be a lover...a great lover. It was music to Jerome's ears. He truly wanted to be a great lover and was eager to learn.

Jerome thought he knew what was coming but was shocked when Diane pushed him onto his back and sucked his dick into her mouth. Jerome's dick was big, hard and throbbing, it was a lot to suck and Diane was somewhat overwhelmed by it, nonetheless she stayed with it. Sucking it deep into her throat and pumping it with her hand at the same time. His dick stretched her jaws and nearly gagged her but Diane truly enjoyed giving her student the first real blowjob of his life. Jerome had entered another world. Because of its size, his dick had been licked on a few times but never really sucked until now. He bucked his hips and pulled Diane's hair when the rushing power of climax coursed through his body then exploded into her throat. He was amazed when she swallowed all of it and didn't stop sucking. Diane used her tongue and lips to milk the last drops of juice from Jerome, taking her time and truly enjoying herself. She slowly licked his balls, slid her wet lips up and down the long shaft several times then swirled her tongue around the head before again sucking his young manhood as deep into her throat as she could take it.

When his dick began to grow hard again Diane comfortably positioned herself on the bed and ordered Jerome to pay close attention. She instructed him on the sensitivity of a woman and the need for him to arouse her before trying to fuck. She invited him to fondle and kiss various parts of her body, coaching him on varying pressure and the use of his hands and tongue.

Jerome followed orders and found himself more turned on than ever as Diane explained why his touch and kisses were important and how they made her feel. When his face was close to her pussy, Diane pulled her lips apart then pointed out and explained her clitoris. Jerome was intrigued and excited, he did not know that women had a little pleasure button and eagerly followed instructions to gently lick and suck it. As his deepest passions began to awaken Jerome settled in and sucked Diane clit with a slow gentle rhythm. He liked what he was doing and felt an overwhelming sense of power and pleasure when Diane cried out in obvious delight.

More than satisfied with his performance, Diane repositioned herself and sucked Jerome's dick while he continued to lick and nibble her tingling clit. After several long pleasurable moments Diane eased Jerome's big hard-on from her mouth. She slid free of him then quickly turned around and slid her tongue between his lips sparking a hot, wet lustful kiss.

With her heart beating fast Diane placed one knee on each side of Jerome and for a moment sat on his legs facing him with a big smile. She coached him to go slow then raised her body, reached out and took hold of

Jerome's big dick and slid it in and out of her. Heated passion ripped through Diane as she lowered herself, taking more of Jerome's dick. She leaned back and rode up and down, each time taking him in a little further with each stroke. Without question Jerome had a big dick. It was more than ten inches long, thick, meaty and uncircumcised. It was certainly the biggest dick Diane had ever taken and her juices flowed because she absolutely wanted all of it. Their excitement grew as Jerome's big young meat pushed in deeper and deeper until finally it disappeared completely inside her. For a few moments they paused, both staring at her pussy. Diane felt a triumphant rush! She had all of it inside her. All of it…every hard inch of Jerome's big beautiful black dick was now deep inside her hot pussy.

Jerome was equally excited. This was the first time he had gotten his entire dick inside a woman. Before now he really didn't think any woman could take all of him. He backed out then stroked deep into Diane several times before again pushing all the way inside her, sparking a few moments of serious deep grinding.

Diane trembled then collapsed against Jerome's chest. She covered his mouth with a long wet kiss then grabbed his shoulders and gently rolled over pulling him on top of her. She carefully instructed Jerome in rhythm and technique then humped her pussy to meet his every thrust. She had intended to teach a lesson but quickly surrendered to the overwhelming joy of fucking this hot young man while tripping on his huge dick invading and stretching her. "Just like that," she cried out. "Oh yeah…Jerome! Oh baby…fuck me daddy! Fuck me! Yeah just like that…ooh! Yeah…yeah…come on Jerome! Come on honey...ooh ooh...so good! Fuck me baby...ooh!"

Jerome was amazed and excited. His dick had never been harder or lasted longer and he knew he was really fucking for the first time. It was good! Incredibly good for both so they took their time and truly enjoyed each other. They were moving in perfect unison with Jerome's big dick sliding and grinding deep inside Diane's hot wet pussy causing her to climax repeatedly, which made her even wetter and that caused Jerome's big dick to grow even bigger and push deeper inside her until it throbbed uncontrollably then exploded again and again, filling his teacher with streams of hot semen.

The next morning Diane sucked Jerome as soon as they awoke. After swallowing his juice and sucking him dry, she explained to him that his first climax would come quickly and must be gotten out of the way so he can get down to real business. The second climax was a lot longer coming and gave him more opportunity to enjoy himself and please his woman. A little while later she sucked him again until he was hard then challenged him to take control. Jerome surprised Diane by taking his time, kissing her in all the right places then licking, nibbling and sucking her clit until she climaxed. Though still rough around the edges, he done a creditable job and Diane was plenty wet and wanting more when Jerome pushed his big hard-on into her. He was a good student and proved to his delighted teacher that he had paid attention and learned well. They made serious love until late into the morning, clinging to one another and sharing long passionate kisses before Diane cooked breakfast then sent Jerome happily on his way.

*****

Elliott awoke early Saturday morning a happy man. He shifted slightly then for several moments watched Tasha peacefully sleep. He thought about their first two times together and her rocky transformation. A transformation Elliott hoped was for real and forever. *It was an amazing thing to see a girl grow into a woman in so short a time. Funny how some of the most meaningful things in life happen very quickly,* he thought. Elliott smiled as he remembered how wonderful Tasha's sexy young body had felt. She even tasted delicious. He began to grow hard when he thought about that look in her eyes as she climaxed when he was fucking her and the sounds, yeah the squeals, moans and sucking in her breath when he tongued her to another climax. All things considered it had been a perfect night. Elliott had passionately licked Tasha's clit until her body tensed, arched, then violently shook. His lips felt her pussy briefly quiver then pulsate with rapid involuntary twitches and spasms. It had been a powerful climax, completely overwhelming Tasha. Elliott had continued to lick and suck her clit until she began to calm down. He then held her in his arms, softly kissing, caressing and complimenting her as they drifted in warm afterglow then on to sleep.

Elliott decided to begin this morning the same way last night ended. He carefully repositioned himself then lowered his mouth to Tasha's pussy. She awoke slowly, first in a dreamy state, then to wide-awake reality. Her immediate instinct was to push Elliott away, but she didn't. Lust, searing hot passion, raw need and the sensations rippling through her body caused Tasha to lie back, spread her legs and caress Elliott's head. For several minutes she squealed, whimpered, moaned, called Elliott's name and fought the impulse to say those three words she felt and knew were for real. When her body arched and her hands clutched then twisted the sheets, Elliott quickly shifted his mouth to her lips, kissed her deeply and slid his throbbing manhood into her. Tasha broke the kiss with a scream. Her body was completely electric, never had she been so hot. She held tightly to Elliott, completely absorbed and swept away. Her pleasure was no greater than his while they kissed, caressed and eagerly made love. Elliott was ecstatic. He simply could not get over how good Tasha felt to him. She was incredible! Young, tight, very wet and whatever comes after you pass hot. For a few beautiful minutes the two of them lost themselves to each other, smoothly fucking to dual climax with such desire, excitement and raw passion that it completely exhausted them.

Elliott awoke the second time to the smell of coffee. He followed the aromas to the kitchen and was delighted to discover Tasha had cooked his breakfast. She had also tidied the house, washed the dishes and cleaned the kitchen. Elliott was impressed and pleased. He leisurely enjoyed his breakfast knowing Tasha was hot...really hot and ready for more sex. He wanted to keep her that way and was determined to do so all day.

"A whole lot of steady fucking in a short period of time leads to burnout and burnout sucks. It's best when you just gotta have it. When you can't stand it no more. Trust me baby we got a whole lot of lovemaking to do. And we will do it on cue and to the max!" he assured.

"What's the cue?" Tasha questioned.

"Come here," Elliott responded.

Tasha snuggled into Elliott's embrace and they caressed, nuzzled, kissed, smoked weed, snacked, watched a movie and became friends. Tasha was floating in a whole new world. A tiny bit of apprehension still lived within her, but for the first time in her adult life, she was relaxed and happy...and in love. She had come full circle with this man. From complete disrespect to awe, admiration and finally love.

She was literally on fire for him and was ready to explode when he began making love to her late Saturday evening. Elliott excited and thrilled her beyond any limit she had previously known. He withheld nothing using his words, hands, tongue, lips and manhood to ignite her deepest passions and drive away her juvenile inhibitions. He liberated and freed Tasha, allowing her to seize control and slam her pussy to him or sit on top and ride him deep in and out while looking into his eyes. To feel a peak building, getting stronger, exciting and good...so unbelievably good. To feel her body shudder while electric sensations seize the whole of her being in one sweet mind blowing rush. Climax! Human explosion! That all to brief, but oh so intense sweet moment when all your nerve ending tingle with waves of pleasure so good you damn near can't stand it. To cum and keep cumming! Tasha was there, peaking with a powerful climax when Elliott came deep inside her. For a short moment they rode the same wave, sharing a rare and precious moment in human relationships. Nothing else mattered as each smothered the other with caresses until sleep finally claimed them.

Sunday morning they slept late, had sex in the shower, ate breakfast then went for a walk. When they returned, Tasha collected her things and Elliott drove her home. She sat close to him in the car, he liked that and she was pleased. He kissed her at a stoplight then massaged her knee while she rested her head on his shoulder, actually wondering what his dick would feel like in her mouth. When Elliott stopped in front of Tasha's house, the kiss good-bye was long and passionate. Her heart was still beating out of rhythm as she watched him drive away then slowly walked into the house. No one was home so she left the house, crossed the street and went to Louise's house.

Jerome stood at the end of the block and watched Tasha cross the street. He was happy; Miss D had turned him out and helped put him on the road to true self-discovery. He now considered himself to be a man, he was moving on with his life and had no use for Tasha. He didn't want to see her and didn't want her to see him. When she disappeared into Louise's house, Jerome continued on his way smiling, singing and plotting his next sexual conquest.

Late on that same Sunday night Elliott lay in bed wide awake. He stared at the ceiling and thought about Tasha. He was proud of Tasha's progress and proud of his efforts in getting her there. Actually, he had accomplished his mission and there really was no reason for a fourth date. Hum...no reason but one hell of a need. He was uncomfortable with the fact that he really liked Tasha. He could not deny that she had delivered the most intense sexual pleasure of his life, but he attempted to blow that off by thinking that passion would lessen with familiarity. What really bothered him was Tasha herself. Something about her was special. She could really be special with proper guidance and just a little work. "Yeah then she would really be special all right...but special only to one man," Elliott spoke aloud. "Lucky sumbitch! Should be me...hell I done the work! Naw...that's nuts...but she can be a close friend. Hum...maybe not, gotta put Diane into this picture somewhere." Elliott struggled with his thoughts for sometime before deciding to concentrate on the present and make the fourth date an experience Tasha would never forget. He then spent another thirty-eight minutes planning the perfect super date before drifting off to sleep.

The following Friday, Tasha took half the day off from work then rushed home to fidget and pace around the house waiting for Elliott. Diane was slightly agitated by it all. While she was thrilled with the change in Tasha's behavior, she knew her daughter was falling head over heels in love. Diane was confident Elliott would let Tasha down gently but it complicated things. How could she listen to her daughter pine away for her lost love then spend the night with that same man. She hoped Elliott would somehow take Tasha beyond that puppy love on this last date and she was relieved when Tasha squealed then dashed out of the house the moment Elliott's car arrived.

Elliott had planned the entire weekend and they followed his plan to the letter. First he took Tasha to an upscale beauty salon for the "treatment." Hair washed and restyled, manicure, pedicure and a complete facial including professional make-up. Next to a stylish boutique and into a sexy tight fitting party dress complete with shoes, handbag, faux pearl earrings and necklace. Tasha began the evening as a sexy young girl but a beautiful classy woman stepped out of the dressing room. An elegant knockout Elliott was proud to have on his arm. He escorted Tasha to an upscale restaurant for the best dinner of her life then on to three different nightclubs, dancing and partying until late in the night. Upon arriving at Elliott's house they were exhausted but fixed drinks, smoked a joint and made love before quickly falling asleep.

*****

Diane also had plans for the weekend. After leaving her daughters and Tasha's baby at her mother's house, she headed straight to the guesthouse. The guesthouse was a converted garage behind Randall Stewart's house. Randall's brother Frank stayed in the guesthouse when he was mad at his wife. He would move in, call Diane and swear his marriage was over. Frank was generous and funny. When she was with him Frank lavished money and attention on Diane and to her delight he was always horny. Diane enjoyed spending time with Frank and arrived at the guesthouse feeling good but found it empty. In spite of the fact he had invited Diane to an exciting evening in the guesthouse Frank abruptly changed his mind without telling her. It wasn't the first time it had happened before and Diane was sick of it. Frank would leave his wife and pledge his love to Diane then after a few weeks he would go back to attending his church then shortly afterwards move back in with his wife.

"I'm through! I've had it! No more!" Diane declared to herself. "His little short ass better stay with his wife cause he ain't getting nothing here. No way! Nothing...I'm tired of being used...I got feelings too!" Diane went home and attempted to drown her hurt with liquor. She did not like to be alone but Frank had crapped out on her and Elliott was busy playing with her daughter. "It ain't fair!" Diane wailed aloud. "I'm all alone! Ain't got nobody...while Tasha is having big fun with my man. That shit ain't right, if she wasn't in my way I could be having fun with Elliott tonight...but naw...I'm all alone."

Diane found herself longing for Eddie. Eddie Thompson was the love of her life. They met several years ago on the job. Both were married at the time but were strongly attracted to each other. In only a few short months their affair blossomed but over a few long years their marriages failed. After his divorce Eddie followed his heart and took a job driving a tractor trailer truck across the country. Eddie loved the open road and only got to town about twice a month. He also loved Diane, carried her picture and dearly wanted her to ride with him. The thought of traveling excited Diane and she really wanted to go but couldn't until her youngest daughter graduated from high school. That was almost three years away so Diane was agitated and fast becoming more so. *Now I'm gonna have to replace Frank,* she thought. *Hum...might have to replace Elliott too. Damn! That ain't good!*

Diane freshened her drink then lounged on her bed. "I may be all alone tonight but I wasn't alone last weekend," She spoke aloud then chuckled. "I had something special, real special," she continued. "A muscular young stud with the biggest meat I've ever had and he had the energy to keep that big thing hard. Hard and hot just for me. Once I got him on the right track that shit was good...real good. Matter-of-fact I wouldn't mind having some more that...and I'm entitled to it. Tasha don't want him, she threw him out and is having big fun with my man. Truth is both of them needed life lessons and Tasha is getting more than one, so it's only right that Jerome get more than one lesson too. Hum...if I play this thing right Jerome can become my regular. Tasha done went and fell in love with Elliott so he ain't likely to choose me over her...course I knew that from the start. But it's all okay now cause Jerome is big enough to replace both Frank and Elliott...ha-ha-ha."

*****

Saturday morning when Elliott awoke Tasha was not in the bed. He smelled coffee, went to the kitchen and made love to her while she giggled, moaned and struggled to prepare breakfast. After the breakfast dishes were washed, Elliott produced a picnic basket, which he and Tasha quickly filled then set off for a long drive, deep into the countryside. They left the car and hiked through the woods to a remote meadow with a small stream meandering through it. Totally separated from the world, they picked wild flowers, splashed naked in the stream, ate, smoked, talked, drank good wine and made love in the great outdoors. Tasha could barely contain herself. She loved this man. He was removing the blinders, allowing her to see, touch and enjoy a small part of the pleasures life has to offer. He had totally blown her mind and was helping her to construct a fresh new perspective.

When they left the meadow and returned to the city, Tasha fully expected to return to Elliott's house but he stopped and checked them into a luxury adult motel. To her complete amazement their room was the ultimate love nest. It was a large room with a fireplace; a stocked wet bar, large screen TV with adult movies, a round bed that vibrated and a Jacuzzi. Tasha was truly impressed with the room, but the Jacuzzi drew her immediate attention. She had never been in a Jacuzzi and Elliott seemed to know that. He encouraged her to give it a try then allowed her to discover its pleasures alone for a short while before joining her. They played vigorously for a while before Tasha briefly settled into Elliott's arms then floated away to relax and enjoy the bubbling water. Several minutes later they emerged from the tub, dressed in the big soft robes provided by the motel then settled into the overstuffed chairs. Elliott snapped on the TV and channel surfed until he found an adult movie. This was another first for Tasha so they watched two adult movies from start to finish.

By early evening Tasha was feeling pampered and wonderfully spoiled. They had enjoyed a delicious steak dinner delivered by room service and served before the fireplace, followed by after dinner drinks in the Jacuzzi. The hot bubbling water was truly a pleasure, the vintage brandy was excellent and Tasha fought to keep from screaming with joy. But after a few minutes she was ready to get out of the tub. She wanted to snuggle and make love to Elliott and the water got in the way.

Elliott gave Tasha a brief sensual massage as he toweled her dry then afterwards she toweled him. She attempted to give him a massage in return but quickly gave up and wrapped her hand around his manhood then pumped it up and down. It stiffened and a single drop of clear fluid glistened from the head of it. She then used both hands and slowly pumped it several more times before lowering her head and lightly kissing the shaft. For a long moment she stared into Elliott's eyes before parting her lips and letting the head of his dick slip into her mouth. Tasha was startled by the waves of pleasure that swept over her as she sucked first just the head then more of him. It was a powerful feeling and she quickly grew wild, nearly out of control, but Elliott patiently calmed, guided and instructed her. When he became satisfied with Tasha's performance, Elliott repositioned his body and covered her pussy with his mouth, introducing her to the unbelievable delights of that well-known position called sixty-nine.

Tasha sucked Elliott's dick almost to the point of gagging then backed off and sucked it in again. She was completely amazed, not only did she really like it, she liked tripping on the feelings it created within her even more. The sense of power and control, the white-hot passion and pure raw lust that caused rippling sensations and juices to flow while her body quivered with absolute delight. She climaxed with a fury grinding her pussy into Elliott's mouth while she continued to explore his dick and balls with her mouth. When Elliott's smooth hard dick entered Tasha's excited pussy she promptly experienced the second of the five orgasms this day and night held in store for her.

Elliott was focused only on the present. And...at this particular moment of the present he had a trophy. A beautiful young female student now passing her final exam with honors. He was pleasantly shocked when she sucked his dick. He hadn't expected her to but he knew what it meant. He had endured great pain and pleasure in guiding and teaching her. Now he was reaping the rewards, tripping just at the sight of her hot saucy lips sucking his dick. He fought back his cum twice, just so he could fuck her and fuck her he did. The bed vibrated, Tasha wailed and Elliott fucked her with all the skill and passion he possessed. Finally locked in tight embrace, all but melted together they soared in climax then drifted into that sweet foggy ecstasy that settles over lovers until peaceful sleep snatches them away.

Sunday morning Elliott awoke hot and excited, he quickly became aware that Tasha was sucking his dick, he was startled...but happy. "I wanted to wake you like you woke me," she purred then went back to sucking. Elliott smiled big and blew her a kiss while he relaxed and enjoyed every second of it. After a few minutes Elliott attempted to pull Tasha into his arms but she refused and sucked him until his cum exploded into her mouth then splashed onto his stomach.

Following a quick shower Elliott ordered breakfast then cuddled with Tasha until the room service waiter arrived. After eating they changed location from the bed to the Jacuzzi for more. More kissing, holding, squeezing, nibbling, sucking, licking and more raw lusty sex. Lost in the passion of making love to a hot young woman in a hot tub, Elliott had a firm grip on Tasha's ass cheeks as she straddled his lap and rode him. He dipped a finger into a nearby jar or hair oil then spread Tasha's cheeks wide and pushed his greasy finger into her asshole, causing Tasha to freeze. She stared at Elliott with wide eyes, then slowly began to grind her ass on his finger. He slid it in and out then pushed two fingers into her and she squealed, "Ooooh! I like that! Ooooh...Elliott. That's nasty...and it hurts a little. But...don't stop...don't..."

Elliott fucked her pussy and fingered her asshole for several moments then shifted their position, eased his dick out of her pussy and into her ass.

"Ohhh! Oh God! Wait! Slowly baby, go slow," Tasha wailed. "Ohhh! Aughhh! Yes...yes...oh Elliott! Elliott! Oh God! I love you Elliott...I love you!" she confessed.

Her virgin ass was extremely tight but very willing. Elliott patiently massaged her body, kissed her neck and whispered into her ear, while his dick pushed deeper into her. When he felt her relax, he slowly pushed the entire length of his dick all the way up her ass and held it there. She moaned loudly, totally freaking out and loving it. This was something Tasha had never even imagined...yet it was happening. She could not describe her feelings. It was wild...fabulous...ten plus-plus! Elliott's dick felt huge and freaky. She squeezed her ass, felt a rush and shuddered. Elliott began using his fingers at the proper places on her pussy while stroking in and out of her ass and in but a few short moments it got wild. They were all over the hot tub, out of it then back in. Pleasing each ther beyond belief before happily collapsing on the bed.

In the early afternoon they checked out of the motel, had lunch at an outdoor cafe then finally returned to Elliott's house. Happy and very pleased with the time they had shared, they drank a toast to their final date, smoked a joint then sat on Elliott's bed and talked for more than two hours. They talked as teacher to student, lover to lover, man to woman and human to human. It was such a deep intimate personal conversation they could not part ways until they undressed and pleased each other one more time.

Just before sunset Tasha stepped from the shower and applied her makeup just as the professional at the salon had suggested. She carefully styled her hair then slipped into her beautiful new party dress, shoes and jewelry. For a few moments Tasha stood transfixed before a full-length mirror. She liked what she saw and blushed hard at her own image...a completely new image...a completely new person...ready for a new life. She collected her things then snuggled close to Elliott, soaking up his many compliments as he drove her home.

Chapter four

D_iane was speechless_ while her daughters were immediately jealous when Tasha walked into the house following her final date with Elliott. The professional makeover was exactly what Tasha needed to complete her transformation into adulthood and Diane's eyes filled with tears as for the first time she truly saw her oldest child as a grown woman. She was pleased and very happy with the change in Tasha and grateful to Elliott for his help but she suspected there was still something going on between them.

According to Tasha it was over and she would be forever grateful to Elliott but was moving on with her life. She shared every detail of her super-date with Elliott and honestly told Diane how special and grown-up it all made her feel. Elliott had shown her a new world then told her it was only a tiny bit of the good life. He went on to tell her she was smart and could have as much of the good life as she was willing to sacrifice for. Good looks were a big plus but to really live a good life you need to posses something people will pay for and that means a skill or education because a good income is vital to living the good life.

Much to Diane's surprise and pleasure, over the next two weeks Tasha rearranged her work schedule then enrolled in a two-year Associate Degree program at the local community college. Tasha was busy, happy and no longer totally preoccupied with sex but Diane was still suspicious. There was no way Elliott and Tasha could go as far as they did then just walk away from it. Elliott had never taken her on no fancy dates or anything even close to what he lavished on Tasha, so she was sure they were pretending it was all over for her sake, but pretending wasn't necessary. Diane had new ambitions and having Tasha hanging out with Elliott made things a whole lot easier. Since she didn't want to appear to be pushing Tasha she decided to take the matter up with Elliott. But Eddie would be in town this coming weekend so Elliott and her new plans would have to wait until next week.

The following Sunday morning Elliott sat up in his bed and smiled at the lady softly sleeping next to him. He liked her. She was in tune with his vibe and reached him at a deeper level. She was sexy, fun and openly admired him in a fashion that turned him on. She brought no demands, agenda or any hidden motives with her, which provided Elliott with some much-needed mental peace in the short time he had known her. She had called him three days after his last date with Tasha, just when he was beginning to feel lonely. But, he didn't want to call any of his lady friends, not so soon after Tasha. Tasha was a stone fox with a young brick house body, a tough act to follow. It wouldn't be fair to invite a lady over and not really be into her, he just needed a little time to recuperate but it wasn't easy. He had done what was asked and brought Tasha into the light then cut her loose, but the thoughts he had of keeping her where beginning to gnaw at him when the phone rang.

Louise Wilson introduced herself by explaining that she was a neighbor and close friend of Diane and Tasha. She advised that she was greatly impressed with Elliott's tutoring of Tasha and offered her congratulations. She was also concerned about him and wondered that after giving so much of himself did he now need a diversion. Someone to channel his thoughts and feeling away from the intensity of his involvement with Tasha. The best remedy for getting over a past lady is a new lady and Louise was willing to be that new lady for as long as needed. Elliott was intrigued and suggested meeting Louise at a coffee shop near his house.

From the instant they sat down together Elliott and Louise were relaxed and very comfortable. They both felt as if they had known the other for a long time and immediately became friends. Horny friends with a very strong mutual attraction. Less than ninety minutes after they met, the two of them were naked and engaging in serious foreplay on Elliott's bed.

Elliott began to grow hard as he thought of their first time. He instantly liked and wanted Louise, then wanted her even more when she confirmed that she wanted him. They had teased and taunted each other in the coffeehouse then got real when they arrived at his place. Louise was tall, slim and light skinned with a short curly afro hairstyle. She was all arms and legs with small firm tits and a small round butt. Compared to Tasha or Diane, Louise almost looked like a little boy but to Elliott she was an exciting breath of fresh air he found intoxicating.

After they undressed and were lying on his bed, Elliott took Louise into his arms and felt his heart beat faster when he touched his lips to hers. The heat and passion of their lingering kiss gently cascaded over the two of them, cementing them into one. For several minutes they kissed, caressed and looked deep into each other's eyes before Elliott pushed his throbbing hard-on into Louise. She was wet but tight and cried out then buried her face into Elliott's neck. Elliott lifted Louise's chin and kissed her softly on the lips. She responded by sucking in his tongue while adjusting her hips so Elliott had better access. He progressed slowly, absolutely enjoying every stroke and delighted to discover that because of her lanky size, Louise was easy to fuck from any angle and she could and did wrap her long legs around him or use them for leverage. He found himself on top of her, her legs and arms securely wrapped around him while his hard dick slid smoothly in and out of her.

She moaned in distinct pleasure then surrendered to the building contractions within her tingling vagina. "I'm gonna...Elliott...Elliott! I'M GONNA CUM BABY!" she wailed.

It was an emotionally powerful moment for Elliott. He exploded in climax inside Louise then held her tight as she sobbed and moaned, gripped in the intense fulfillment of her own physical and emotional release. The intensity and rarity of their mutual release escalated them to a whole new realm, totally exposing their natural compatibility. Far beyond the incredible physical pleasure they shared was a defining mental awareness of just how wonderful and special they would become to each other. Elliott had experienced many lovers in life and Louise only a few, but never had either been so deeply touched or completely satisfied. At that precise moment, without her knowledge or consent, Louise Wilson became that special woman in Elliott's life.

Since that first encounter Louise had become Elliott's most frequent visitor. The first few times she only spent the night but since she worked her job four days on and three days off, this time she had spent all three days off with him. Elliott started to kiss her but stopped short. She was so beautiful and sleeping so peacefully he did not want to wake her. He promised his semi-hard dick that it would slide inside her within only a few minutes, then slowly got out of bed and went to the bathroom. After washing up Elliott returned to bed but Louise was not there. She had awakened, gone to the kitchen to make coffee then stepped into the shower. Elliott was sitting up in bed sipping a cup of coffee when Louise returned.

"What a gorgeous long tall drink of water!" Elliott cooed much to Louise's delight. She settled on the bed and he pulled her into his arms and pressed his lips to hers. She responded with all that she had, silently wishing this man was hers alone. She gasped as Elliott's lips and tongue began to explore her neck and breast and she was breathing hard when they shifted position and Elliott's hungry mouth sucked in her clit. She moaned with satisfied pleasure as she slid Elliott's dick into her mouth and felt her every nerve-ending tingle. Elliott was nearly overwhelmed...this woman was a true delight. Because of her size she was easy and comfortable to be with. He cupped her small butt while vigorously licking her clit and loved every minute of it. He loved the taste and feel of her, loved knowing she loved it, loved the way she was sucking his dick and most of all, he loved getting lost within her until his lips and tongue were suddenly jolted by the violent spasms and contractions of her orgasm. After a few moments Elliott surprised Louise by pulling her out of bed and backing her to the wall. He lifted one of her legs and pushed his throbbing hard-on into her. *Slowly because she is tight*...he mentally coached himself. *Back out a little, then back in...deeper. Out a little, in a little deeper...oh fuck its good. Out again now way deep...oh yeah...yeah!*

Louise hooked her leg around Elliott balanced herself and fucked with joy...standing up. Her height made it easy for Elliott to get inside her and he made the most of it. At times holding her hips and riding her up and down his shaft. Louise could not take her eyes off of Elliott's dick. She loved to watch herself getting fucked, that was something she did not see very often and it was a major turn on. In fact it was too much and too damn good for both of them but they hung on for as long as they could before collapsing onto the bed in a wild finale of furious orgasmic lust.

Following breakfast Louise snuggled in Elliott's arms on the living room sofa. "Damn...I sure hate to go home...I like being with you," she pouted.

"Don't go," Elliott responded.

"Yeah...I wish I could stay, but I gotta get ready for work and touch base with the boys and do stuff...you know?" she questioned.

"Life's full of stuff," Elliott chuckled.

"Yeah I know," Louise agreed, "but it won't be long now. Sometimes I can't believe my baby is almost fifteen."

"You have two boys right?" Elliott questioned.

"Right," Louise confirmed. "Troy, he'll be eighteen in May and Richard will be fifteen this November. I have shared custody with their father and it's getting harder and harder to make them leave his house and come back to mine. They like playing football and sports and stuff and their father does too so they like being together. And that's okay but they need to pay attention to their studies and grades too. Anyway it's a struggle but I'm winning. Troy will graduate right on time next year and Richard will graduate on time too. Once they graduate they can do what they want."

"Do they play sports for their school?" Elliott asked.

"Ha-ha," Louise chuckled, "that's what their father used to get shared custody. He lives closer to their school and both of them are potential scholarship athletes...but enough about them, I'm sure you have enough stuff of your own to deal with from Diane and Tasha."

"I'm not getting any stuff from Tasha or Diane," Elliott responded. "Matter-of-fact I haven't seen either of them since my last date with Tasha. Why should they give me any stuff anyway?"

"Ha-ha..." Louise chuckled. "You really don't know do you?"

"Know what?" Elliott asked.

"They are waiting for you to choose one of them," Louise advised with a twinkle in her eye.

"Choose one of them...for what?" Elliott asked in a confused voice.

"To be your lover," Louise replied. "You have had both of them so now they are expecting you to choose which you prefer to keep on seeing."

"I prefer to keep on seeing both of them," Elliott replied.

"Women are very competitive sweetheart. They are expecting you to choose."

"Hum...I choose to have them both at the same time," Elliott confessed.

"Sorry dear, you're talking about a mother and daughter here and I don't think Diane would even do something like that with me," Louise replied.

"But you wouldn't have a problem with it would you?" Elliott questioned.

"Just what are you asking?" Louise responded.

"Would you have a problem with another woman in the bed with you and me. That's what I'm asking," Elliott explained.

"That depends on the woman and the circumstances," Louise answered.

"Been there before?" Elliott questioned.

"Yes and no," Louise giggled. "I've been there on cocaine with a girlfriend of mine a few years ago. We got high and done her boyfriend then we done each other. It was a major rush of drugs and sex."

"Only once?" Elliott prodded.

"Oh no," Louise confessed. "But we only done her boyfriend twice before we just left him out of it completely."

"You like the taste of a female huh?" Elliott probed.

"I liked that one when I was high on cocaine," Louise confided.

"Had any other women?"

"No...just Katy...I'm not really into chicks, but with Katy and cocaine it's different and can get kinky if we want it to. What about you...how do you feel about another man in the bed?"

"Not something I've considered really but like you said I guess it would depend on the guy and the circumstances," Elliott replied.

"Have you ever tasted a guy?" Louise questioned.

"Hell no!" Elliott snapped. "The only reason for two guys to be in the same bed is to double up on a lady."

"You wouldn't let a guy suck you?" Louise asked.

"Maybe but I wouldn't suck him," Elliott answered.

"Would you screw a guy?" Louise inquired with a smirk.

"Nope...not my idea of a good time and to save you from asking, nope I'm not game to get poked in my booty either," Elliott advised. After a moment of silence they both broke out in laughter and continued to crack up for several moments.

"So are you going to choose Diane or Tasha?" Louise again questioned.

"Hell naw," Elliott responded. "Choosing sounds like making a commitment and I'm not interested in committing to either one of those women."

"Oh really why?" Louise asked.

"You kidding?" Elliott responded. "Tasha's too big a burden and Diane's too big a challenge."

"What do you mean?"

"Look...Tasha is of another generation and she has a very young child. On top of that she is young, fine and got a dynamite body which means she will attract a lot of attention, most of it unwanted. Nothing in that for me but a lot of stress...so no thanks I'll pass. Diane also has children and grandchildren and she has a lot of game. Be hard to close both eyes real tight with Diane around. So nope...nothing there either but stress so once again I'll pass. But hey I'm willing to party..." Elliott offered with a grin.

"What about me I got kids too?" Louise questioned.

"I don't know what to make of you. But...if I got to be choosing somebody you're my number one," Elliott confessed.

"Oh yeah, I'm sure you tell all your women that," Louise responded. "Are you going to tell Diane or Tasha about us?"

"I don't report to Diane or Tasha or anyone else," Elliott advised. "My business is my business, in fact, as long as you continue to come around I'm not going out of my way to look for Tasha or Diane or anyone else. I like you."

"Do you mean that?" Louise questioned with wide eyes.

"Of course I mean it," Elliott assured. "I'm happy to hang out with you...and maybe Katy and the cocaine every now and then."

Louise looked deep into Elliott's eyes searching for his soul. She had contacted him on impulse because she was lonely and high on booze and weed. She was scrolling through her caller ID and discovered his phone number. A number left there by Tasha who frequently used Louise's phone. Louise was a little jealous of Tasha and Diane. Both of those women have big boobs and ample shapely bodies that easily attract men while Louise was tall, skinny and a little plain looking. Men usually looked right past her, at times making her feel invisible. She made the call to Elliott expecting nothing more than a slightly kinky conversation but got more, a whole lot more. Now she was dangerously close to falling in love and seriously wondering if she dared hope Elliott was also falling in love with her. She kissed him several times on the lips then lowered her head and sucked most of his dick into her mouth while tears flooded her eyes.

Late Wednesday evening, Elliott was amused by Diane's insecurity. After offering her sincere thanks for his efforts on behalf of her daughter, she prodded him to admit he found Tasha more attractive and sexier than her. "Each woman brings her own individual thing so I don't try to compare them," Elliott responded.

"Honey you don't have to bullshit me!" Diane countered. "You know you like that sexy young stuff with everything tight and firm! You can say it…hell I ain't mad. Just like you I've been giving a few lessons to a young thing myself so I know what the deal is. You and Tasha don't have to be pretending for my sake and I mean that. Go ahead and hangout all you want to it won't bother me."

"So you hooked-up with a young brother huh?" Elliott questioned with amusement.

"It's a possibility," Diane responded feeling a little uncomfortable with the subject.

"Well tell me about him. What makes this brother special?" Elliott questioned.

"We're getting off the subject," Diane protested.

"No we're not...young stuff is the subject...right?" Elliott responded with a grin. "So what makes your young buck special? Look at you getting all warmed up just thinking about him. So what's the deal?"

"The boy is hung baby," Diane whispered. "I did not know a dick could really be that big or feel that good. I'm sorry baby nothing personal cause you the teacher, but nature was real kind to that boy."

"Shit, nothing I can say to that except enjoy!" Elliott replied.

"So now you understand why you don't have to pretend about how you feel about Tasha," Diane assured.

"I'm not pretending!" Elliott insisted. "Oh never mind! Take off your clothes then get over here and suck my dick!" he ordered.

"Yes sir," Diane responded. Wearing a big smile as she quickly and eagerly followed orders.

Diane left Elliott's house that night feeling great and certain she had cleared the air without burning any bridges. She had held back a little and not made love as good as she could, hoping Elliott would think she was not as good as he remembered and pursue whatever unfinished business he had with Tasha. That would get Tasha out of the house, the other children could be left with her mother and Diane would then have the whole house to herself. Free to entertain Jerome.

It took three evenings of cruising the neighborhood before Diane spotted Jerome leaning against a fence near the basketball courts behind Madison Middle School. She parked nearby then stepped from her car wearing a sexy short skirt and a very low cut blouse. She walked a short distance toward the courts soaking up the catcalls and whistles before she stopped and motioned for Jerome.

"Hey Miss D whazzup?" Jerome questioned. "Damn! You sure looking fine!"

"I've been looking for you Jerome, do you have a few minutes for me?" Diane questioned.

"Shit I got all day for you Miss D," Jerome responded with a big grin.

"Then let's go," Diane suggested.

As she turned to walk back to her car Jerome put his arm around her, mostly to impress the brothers on the court who were still talking stuff and whistling at Diane.

A few blocks down the street Diane pulled over and stopped her car. "Jerome? Do you know why I came looking for you?" she asked.

"I hope so, but no not really," Jerome replied.

"I came looking because I've been worried about you," Diane explained. "You only got one lesson and although I'll admit you were a good student, follow-up is always necessary. I expected to hear from you way before now; you may even need more lessons."

"Damn...I didn't know. Ah...I'm sorry Miss D. I'll try and..." Jerome stammered.

"Never mind baby, I'll forgive you this time," Diane cooed then got down to business. "Now let's get on to scheduling your evaluation. I need to know how to contact you once I have the girls out of the house. Do you have a phone?"

"Yeah I got a phone and I got my own place too!" Jerome bragged.

"What! Naw you don't!" Diane challenged.

"Yeah I do," Jerome insisted, "I live in the Stone Manor Apartments. I've been living there since my mom and step-dad threw me out. Well they really didn't throw me out, I came home one day and my step-dad said, don't set down and don't stop moving, pack-up all your junk right now, cause as of today you live at a different address. Once I got my stuff together he took me to the Stone Manor and paid my first two months rent and I been there every since. I was mad at first and didn't tell nobody where I lived, but I love it now. I pay my own rent and ain't no way I'd move back home."

Diane started the engine of her car, "Well...are you going to invite me over Jerome?" she questioned.

She pretended to be impressed but inside Diane was amused by Jerome's tiny efficiency apartment. Jerome however was beaming with pride as he gave the grand tour. The apartment was one large sparsely furnished room. On each end of the wall facing the entrance was an alcove. In one alcove was a small kitchen while the other contained a large closet, between the alcoves was a small bathroom. Following the short tour, Jerome stepped into the kitchen to make drinks while Diane seated herself on his daybed. She looked around and silently scolded herself for making assumptions about Jerome. She had underestimated him while wasting time and effort. Nonetheless she was glad she found him dressed as she was. All eyes had been on her and every man and boy there, Jerome included, was getting turned on watching her approach the basketball courts. Jerome got a chance to really show off in front of his friends by leaving with her and he was excited to be alone with her tonight. But, he was a single young man with his own apartment, so Diane was certain his time would become limited as his choices for company increased. Tonight she was his first choice and she fully intended to make herself his first choice on any night.

Jerome was thrilled with his unexpected good fortune. Because of the size of his manhood his luck with women was not all that good. His member had scared away or been rejected by many of the women he met and the last two women he had been with both objected. One only agreed to oral sex, which she didn't perform worth a damn, and the other kept scooting away or pushing on his stomach to keep him from penetrating too deep. Neither of them had been satisfying experiences and Jerome was truly ready for some serious loving. Miss D was at the top of his list. She had provided the most exciting and satisfying sexual experience of his young life. An experience he had frequently bragged about and longed to repeat. Miss D was the only woman he had been with who took all of him and truly liked it. She had taken her time and really showed him just what the fuck making love was all about. First she showed him how then she showed him just how good it could be. She did not have to do that and he would always love her for it.

Jerome served two very large and very strong drinks then seated himself next to Diane. They drank a toast to each other and briefly made small talk before their lips touched and their hands began to explore each other's body.

"Jerome," Diane gasped as she broke the kiss, "I want you to do something for me."

"Anything, just name it," Jerome responded.

"I want you to stand out there in the center of the room and undress then pose for me," Diane instructed.

"For real?" Jerome questioned.

"Oh yeah...for real," Diane assured. "I want to take a mental picture of you and I want it to be hot."

"What do you mean by a mental picture?" Jerome questioned.

"Nothing big...just a picture that I see in my mind when I think of you," Diane explained. "Once somebody puts a real pose in your mind that's what you will see whenever you think of them. After you pose for me, I'll pose for you."

Jerome took a large swallow from his drink, flipped on his stereo then stepped to the center of the room and began removing his clothes. He felt a little awkward until Diane called out, "yeah baby...take it all off!" Using the rhythm of the music Jerome completed his striptease then done his best to strike several classic poses, all while Diane cheered him on. Like a big cat moving in for a kill, Diane's eyes were sparkling. She saw Jerome as a delicious piece of young meat and focused hard on his dick. It looked to be even bigger than she remembered and she was sure it wasn't fully hard. Jerome was about six feet tall and weighed around one hundred eighty pounds. He was lean yet muscular and his final pose held Diane spellbound for a few moments before she gave him a standing ovation while shouting, "That's it...that's it baby! Damn...sure wish I had a camera. You one fine young brother! Shit you look like some kind of African King or something...you bad baby...bad!"

Jerome was breathing hard and grinning big when he settled onto the daybed and watched Diane slither out of her clothes then seductively progress from one erotic pose to another. His manhood was hard and throbbing when she danced across the room then stopped close in front of him. Diane slowly lowered herself to her knees, reached out and took Jerome's dick into her hand. Quietly amazed all over again by the size of him she wrapped her other hand around Jerome's dick, putting one hand on top of the other. *Wow!* she thought, *I got two hands full and there is still that much or more left...this is it baby...four hands or better makes this the king of dicks!* She massaged it with her big soft titties then gurgled with pleasure as she stretched her lips around it and began to suck. Jerome was absolutely delighted; nothing could be better than this. He lightly stroked her hair and moaned while Diane gorged and gagged herself trying to suck as much of him as she could. Within a few moments they were lying opposite each other on the bed. Jerome nestled his head between Diane's legs and got busy licking and sucking her clit while she pumped his big hard dick up and down then sucked it into her mouth and swirled her tongue around and around it. The passion of pure lust soon exploded from both of them challenging Diane to try and swallow Jerome's river of cum while her pussy was convulsing in its own powerful climax.

After several minutes of rest and several more minutes of cuddling Jerome began to get hard again. It was exactly what Diane was waiting for. She had happily gotten swept away with the oral sex but getting every bit of that giant dick inside her was what she really came here for. She played with his dick and nibbled at Jerome lips while he ran his hands over her body until she could stand waiting no longer. Diane rose up and straddled Jerome who was lying flat on his back. She guided his dick to her opening then slightly lowered herself onto it. She was anxious and wet but still had to slowly work that big dick into her. After she slid the head of it in and out a few times, Jerome got a firm grip on her hips and began penetrating deeper with each stroke until Diane became slightly overwhelmed and temporarily lightheaded. She collapsed onto his chest feeling as though he was pushing into parts of her that had not previously been touched but she remained determined to take all of him. Jerome lifted her chin then touched his lips to hers while he continued to slowly slide in and out. Their kiss grew wet then demanding and hungry. Diane held Jerome's head with both hands while her tongue searched his and her hips pumped up and down in an effort to get even more of his big hard-on inside her. Suddenly Diane cried out as her pussy involuntarily contracted from the incredible pleasure of fucking this giant dick. She sat up, leaned back and placed her hands behind her on Jerome's legs then looked down. Most of his dick was inside her, most but not all, so Diane began riding up and down. Jerome held firm to her hips and smoothly stroked to her rhythm until his entire dick disappeared from view. She squealed with delight then leaned forward as did Jerome and they hugged each other while deep grinding and kissing. Diane marveled at the sensation of being completely full of dick. She felt invaded and penetrated beyond permissible limits yet every nerve ending within her tingled at the slightest movement of that giant dick. It was a gloriously freaky feeling that slowly swept all over her body and made her even hotter. After several moments Jerome gently rolled Diane onto her back without slipping out. She raised her legs and Jerome went to work. He pushed in deep then pulled almost out before pushing his big dick deep into Diane again and again. She violently thrashed her hips and wailed as Jerome rose up, rode his big dick all the way inside her and fucked hard, causing Diane's legs to go weak and her pussy to contract and spasm in a mind numbing climax. When his toes curled and his body grew tense, Jerome held Diane tight and rocked deep inside her as cum exploded from his swollen dick in a furious and deeply satisfying rush.

Exhausted but still horny they lay in each other's arms for several minutes nuzzling and kissing.

"I sure hate it, but we gonna have to finish this tomorrow baby," Diane advised.

"Damn...I was hoping you was gonna spend the night," Jerome responded.

"I'd sure love to and I will, but we gonna have to plan that out. For right now though we still got some unfinished business for tomorrow don't we baby?" Diane cooed.

"Damn straight we do!" Jerome quickly agreed.

"Good I'll be here around seven-thirty," Diane advised.

"You a real special lady Miss D, most women I done met can't even take half my dick," Jerome flatly stated. It was meant and received as a compliment.

"Let me tell you something baby," Diane responded. "Don't ever forget that you got the king of dicks...the king. The king must be worshipped baby, so any bitch that can't take all of it, don't deserve none of it. You remember that, I'm your teacher and my pussy is your queen but it is also the king's slave in worship when it is serving you...and it must serve you well...all of you! Do you understand what I'm saying?" she questioned.

"Yeah...that's some deep shit!" Jerome replied. "You really mean you're my queen?" he asked.

"No not me!" Diane corrected. "My pussy is queen to your dick. It treats it right, takes it all and sets the standard for any other woman. And it will be there for you to fuck! Not everyday, not even every week, but the queen will be there for the king baby...all of the king! Now take the king out of me so I can get on home," she chuckled.

Chapter five

*T*asha *relaxed on Elliott's couch* and sipped her drink. This was only the second time she had visited him in the ten months since their last formal date. She was poised and happy; a completely different young lady from the one Elliott first met. Tasha had been deeply touched and affected by the many good things Elliott showed and taught her about life. He was the reason she had turned her life completely around and was now nearing completion of her first year of college. Once she discovered that a little honest effort paid off with good grades, Tasha poured herself into her classes and was on track to complete her degree requirements right on schedule.

"I hope you don't mind me just popping up out of nowhere but I had to see you," Tasha explained.

"You kidding?" Elliott chuckled. "I was delighted when you called." He was dressed in his favorite pair of silk pajamas and they did not escape Tasha's notice.

"Can I put on one of your pajama tops?" she asked.

It was music to Elliott's ears. He hurried to his closet and collected the silk pajama top that had been Tasha's favorite.

"Oh wow! You remembered...you're so sweet," Tasha gushed. "Now I can get comfortable. I like being with you because I can relax with no pressure and be myself."

She quickly undressed while Elliott watched with lustful admiration. *No question about it Tasha is a stone fox,* he thought to himself, *long black hair, beautiful soft olive skin, big perky titties that screamed to be caressed a narrow waist and a perfectly round firm butt with nicely tapered legs. Damn that's one fine young sister! No wonder I had such a hard time letting her go. Hum...good thing Louise came along or this whole thing might have ended differently.*

"Now where was I?" Tasha questioned as she snuggled back into the couch.

"Maybe about to light this," Elliott suggested as he handed her a joint.

Tasha took several drags from the joint, finished her drink then handed the joint back to Elliott as she got up and made another drink.

"I haven't been really loaded in a long time," Tasha confessed, "but tonight I'm really going to get fucked up."

"Any special reason why?" Elliott asked.

"Oh yeah...there's always a reason," Tasha chuckled.

"Want to tell me about it?" Elliott prodded.

"I met somebody," Tasha replied.

"Well that's a good thing isn't it?" Elliott suggested.

"Yes...except for one thing and that is you!" Tasha responded.

"Me?" Elliott questioned.

"Yes you," Tasha confirmed. "I'll be doing just fine, going on with my life then all of a sudden I start thinking about you and I just gotta be with you. That's what was going on the last time I visited. After we've been together I'm okay for quite a while. Now I've met somebody I have real feelings for but I'm afraid to commit to him if I still have feelings for you."

"Hey baby, you can't let past relationships stand in the way of your future," Elliott advised. "You gotta exorcise them demons...even if it's me."

"I guess that's what I'm hoping to do tonight," Tasha surmised.

"So you think this thing could get really serious huh?" Elliott questioned.

"Yes I do," Tasha responded. "And it's funny you know, I used to date this guy awhile back and he's like a completely different person now. I ran into him at school and could not believe he was actually inside a school, but there he was. He's enrolled in an electrical engineering program and it's amazing the things we now have in common. He really gets along well with Kayla, that's my daughter, and we have talked about becoming a family and supporting each other."

"Hum...sounds like a done deal to me," Elliott replied.

"Not until he proposes," Tasha corrected.

"You holding out for the real deal huh?" Elliott questioned.

"And you know it!" Tasha responded with a big smile. "You're the one who told me marriage was the ultimate commitment and if I'm going to be in a committed relationship, I can't accept less."

"You sure you can successfully add another level of responsibility?" Elliott questioned. "Seems to me you already have a job, school and a young daughter. A husband will also need time and attention."

"We have talked about that but because we are both working and going to school we should have a more balanced life and a brighter future hanging together than we would living apart. We can save money on some things and not have to worry about a social life, so in a way it should all even out," Tasha responded.

"Fine as you are I'm surprised he hasn't asked already," Elliott declared.

"Our break-up wasn't pretty way back when so it has taken a little time for us to get to know each other all over again. Plus we have both grown up a lot and started to take life more seriously. Shoot...college makes you serious whether you want to be or not," Tasha explained as she fixed both of them another drink.

"So you are growing, life is good and you have no problems, is that what I am hearing?" Elliott asked with a smile.

"No...you are still a problem," Tasha pouted.

"Oh I think you'll get over that pretty quickly after you become a wife," Elliott assured.

"You sound so certain, how can you be so sure?" Tasha asked.

"Cause I don't mess with no married women...that's how!" Elliott responded.

Tasha giggled then sat down on Elliott's lap, looked into his eyes and touched her lips to his.

*****

Three months later just after the start of the New Year, Diane was daydreaming about being on the road with Eddie while cleaning her kitchen and humming a happy tune. It had been a good year for Diane and she was looking forward to another. She had just spent the weekend with Eddie, who to her delight, was getting to town a lot more often. A secondary delight for Diane was the fact that Frank's wife threw him out for good about four months after he last stood her up. He was now permanently living in the guesthouse and she was now the one who occasionally stood him up. Jerome had become harder to catch up with as she knew he would, and she had only seen Elliott twice because she was sure he was seeing Tasha and they were being quiet about it.

Diane had just removed several odds and ends from the refrigerator when Tasha burst into the house full of excitement about her newly acquired engagement ring.

"I'm not surprised, not a bit," Diane proclaimed. "I knew if you and Elliott kept fooling around something like this could happen."

"Elliott?" Tasha questioned. "I'm not engaged to Elliott I'm going to marry Jerome."

"Jerome? You mean the same Jerome you ran out of this house with a gun?" Diane questioned.

"That was a long time ago mom we have both grown up a lot since then," Tasha responded.

"Aw naw...hell naw!" Diane wailed. "Girl you can't be serious. After all the shit we went through with that boy, how could you even think of seeing him again...let alone talk about marrying him!"

"He has changed mom, we both have. I ran into him in school and I was shocked. But he is serious. He works days and goes to school in the evening just like I do. We started talking and I was really impressed with how much he has matured and one thing just led to another. I think we still had strong feelings for each other, we must have, or we wouldn't be so close now," Tasha explained.

"So what happened between you and Elliott?" Diane questioned.

"I love Elliott and I will always be grateful to him but he's too old for me. Jerome is a lot closer to my age and Elliott is really not interested in a relationship with me anyway," Tasha replied.

"Did he say that?" Diane asked.

"Yes...he said we were at different places in life and while we could enjoy each other at the intersections, we were still traveling different roads. So I should be true to myself and do what is best for me," Tasha responded.

"And you think that is marrying Jerome?" Diane questioned.

"Jerome and I talked about getting married because we are in love and have so much in common. We both want to make a serious effort to have and become something. We want to become a family, spend our time together and be there for each other. But, I was still surprised when he finally popped the big question tonight," Tasha declared with a big smile.

Diane collapsed into a chair and stared open mouth at her daughter for several moments. Then she quietly asked, "Have you showed your ring to Louise?"

"Not yet," Tasha responded.

"Then why don't you run across the street and show her. I need time to let this shit soak in!" Diane declared. "I just can't believe you right back where we started."

"We're not mom...not even close. Elliott took me to school and somehow Jerome got some real good schooling too. We're light years beyond where we were. I think we were right for each other all along, we just needed to grow up," Tasha declared.

"Uh-huh," Diane responded. "Go on and talk to Louise, I still need some time to swallow this."

The following evening, Diane sat in her car with growing impatience until Jerome arrived at home. She watched him enter the building then followed a few minutes later.

Jerome was shocked when Diane stormed into his apartment demanding to know if he had lost his mind. "How the hell could you have the nerve to be seeing Tasha and me at the same time? Then turn around and ask her to marry your ass?" Diane demanded.

"I thought you knew me and Tasha was seeing each other," Jerome explained.

"Like hell!" Diane fumed. "Ain't neither one of you told me shit! And you low enough to be in bed with both of us."

"It ain't like that's something new Miss D," Jerome advised. "And you said yourself that your pussy was queen to my king dick. The queen sets the standard and it will be there for me, not every day or even every

week but it will be there. So you knew I would be
hooking up with other women. But when I saw Tasha in
school, I realized that I really didn't want no other
woman. Tasha is a princess and comes closer than any
other woman to the standard set by my queen. I could
settle for nothing less than this beautiful princess I love
and it is only right for a king to have royal women share
his life. It will be a lot easier for the queen to find
comfort when she knows the king is nearby and that the
princess is happy."

"Uh-huh…you think you really got it going on
don't you?" Diane accusingly asked.

"Yes! Absolutely!" Jerome declared. "I love you
and I will always be grateful for what you done for me
Miss D and that is a good thing. When I ran into Tasha
at school I realized that way down inside I truly love
her. She is and will always be my princess. You are and
will always be my queen. So it is only natural for me to
ask for her hand and your understanding."

It had been a few months since she had last seen
Jerome and Diane was greatly impressed with his
maturity and improved verbal skills. She wanted to be
tough with him but found herself being seduced by his
words and growing horny for his touch despite the fact
she really did not come to his apartment for that reason.

"Just what kind of understanding you expect
from me?" she asked trying to sound stern.

"The kind that keeps things between us. Strictly
and only between us!" Jerome explained.

"What makes you think there will be anything to
keep?" Diane snapped.

"Because I am the king…and there is already
something to keep," Jerome advised with a sly smile.

Diane was quickly losing the battle. She wanted and didn't want Jerome at the same time. She knew he was implying that they were already dirty so there was no reason why their relationship could not continue. She tried to get sex out of her mind and change the subject but Jerome took off his shirt, loosened his belt and stepped out of his pants.

"And...just as the queen herself has declared," Jerome announced as he stepped from his underwear, "the king must be worshipped!" He stood naked before her with his big thick dick getting bigger as it grew hard.

In spite of herself Diane gave in to her agonizing lust, hoping she would have better luck keeping her desires under control in the future. She silently vowed to never be alone with Jerome after this night then whispered, "You are right my lord, the king must be worshipped." She quickly undressed then knelt before him and shuddered as tingling sensations raced throughout her body when she reached out and stretched her lips around her future son-in-law's big hard dick.

Jerome could not have been happier. He had been very concerned about his relationship with Miss D. While he loved Tasha and wasn't going to let anything come between them, his only worry had been this thing with her mom. But Miss D was really cool and fulfilling his wish to have both of them permanently. He watched with pride as his dick grew in size while Miss D happily sucked it. After several moments Jerome placed Diane on his daybed. He kissed her passionately, pleased with the knowledge that she remained firmly within his control. He took his time arousing and pleasing her before slowly sliding his throbbing hard-on into her hot and very wet womanhood. Diane cried out and clutched at Jerome as his big dick pushed deeper and deeper into her. She tossed her head from side to side totally swept up in the heat and passion of this fabulous lover she helped create. She was nearing the peak of her climax when Jerome exploded inside her causing Diane to scream with delight and cling tightly to this young man she truly adored and in spite of herself, could not resist.

*****

On a warm Saturday afternoon in early spring, Diane, Tasha and Louise sat on Diane's back porch sipping lemonade and planning Tasha's wedding. Because the wedding was going to be small most of the details were simple. The biggest problem for Tasha was deciding who would give her away. She did not know her birth father and did not get along well with her ex-stepfather.

"I asked Big Poppa but he said he had bad feet and couldn't stand up very long," Tasha pouted. "Then he said I should ask Uncle Henry to do it."

"What did Henry say?" Diane asked.

"I didn't ask him," Tasha replied. "He's always drunk...I don't want no drunk giving me away."

"I feel you on that?" Louise agreed. "The man that gives you away should be someone you respect."

"You got some cousins that would be happy to help out," Diane suggested.

"Naw...I know who I'll ask. I'll get Elliott to give me away...I mean...he was my teacher in a way and I do respect him a lot," Tasha declared.

"Ha-ha..." Louise chuckled. "Elliott ain't gonna do that."

Both Diane and Tasha put their drinks down and stared at Louise.

"Just how do you know what Elliott ain't gonna do?" Diane questioned.

Louise swallowed hard; she realized her remark may have let the cat out of the bag so she faced it head on. "He and I have a close personal relationship," Louise confessed.

After a brief silence Diane erupted in laughter, "You and Elliott...ah...ha-ha-ha-ha..."

Tasha also found Louise's ridiculous claim just as funny and joined in the infectious laughter, which soon also drew in Louise.

Yet, only a few days later Louise was nestled comfortably in Elliott's arms while they watched a movie. Their relationship had flourished and she now felt very secure...even loved, as did Elliott.

"Can you believe Tasha came by her a couple days ago and asked me to give her away at her wedding?" Elliott asked after the movie ended and he snapped off the television.

"Are you going to do it?" Louise questioned.

"Hell naw, weddings are not my thing and I ain't her daddy," Elliott responded.

"Did you tell her that?"

"Naw I told her I would think about," Elliott replied.

"It won't kill you," Louise chuckled.

"Yeah...but why me? I mean that's just weird."

"She respects you and doesn't have a father, what's so weird about that? After all you were her teacher in a way, so it's reasonable for you to stand in for her dad," Louise explained.

"I don't know...it just seems to me that the man giving a woman away should not have slept with her," Elliott responded.

"Baby this will be far from a storybook wedding," Louise chuckled. "Your giving Tasha away may be the most normal part of it."

"I don't know. I'm still not comfortable with it," Elliott insisted.

"Hey baby it's only a few minutes on an ordinary Saturday afternoon. A special favor for a good friend before a few strangers...simple as that," Louise advised.

"You're right; it's really not that big a deal is it?" Elliott questioned.

"No it's not..." Louise agreed with a growing smile.

"Okay I'll call Tasha and tell her she's on...I'll do it! You know something?" Elliott asked.

"What?"

"I don't mind giving Tasha away but I'll never part with you," he replied with sincerity then tightly hugged Louise.

*****

Much to his surprise, Elliott found himself to be somewhat nervous as he stood next to Tasha. They were waiting for their cue to pass through the inner doors of the church and proceed down the aisle to the altar. He looked at Tasha and she held his gaze, her eye's searching his in a way he found uncomfortable. "You look absolutely gorgeous! Just way too beautiful for words," he reassured her then straightened his tie as a way of breaking eye contact.

"I love you," Tasha whispered just as the doors swung open and the organ began the introduction to the wedding march.

The small crowd rose to their feet as Tasha and Elliott stepped through the doors and began their march to the altar. Tasha floated down the aisle in a glorious fog. It was as if she were in the midst of an absolutely wonderful, yet surreal dream. She had really loved only two men in her short life and today one was giving her away to the other.

Elliott was greatly relieved to get to the altar without incident. It wasn't easy to walk beside a woman wearing a big dress. He was even more relieved when the pastor finally asked, "Who giveth this woman to be wed?"

"I do on behalf of the Reynolds family sir," Elliott responded, then placed Tasha's hand into Jerome's.

"Thank you. You may be seated," the pastor instructed.

Though he was not the one getting married, Elliott was lightly perspiring when he took his designated seat next to Diane. It had been years since he had been anywhere near a wedding and he was not enjoying this one. He closed his eyes and took a deep breath then was shocked when Diane took his hand and began massaging her inner thigh with it, all while the bride and groom were exchanging vows. Elliott snatched his hand away giving Diane an indignant look that caused her to blush but behave.

Immediately following the ceremony the reception was held in the basement of the church. Elliott done his duty in the receiving line, watched the cake cutting, offered a toast and presented the bride and groom with a gift then saw little reason to stick around.

The x-rated deal between mother and daughter was now complete, but in a way neither of them could have possibly imagined. So while Tasha, Jerome and Diane posed for yet another picture, Elliott collected his coat and gloves then reached out and collected his woman, putting his arm around Louise as the two of them strolled out of the church. That particular picture would show Jerome with a huge smile, standing in the middle with his right arm around his new wife and left arm around his new mother-in-law, but the two women were both staring past the camera wearing looks of shocked disbelief.

www.ingramcontent.com/pod-product-compliance
Lightning Source LLC
Chambersburg PA
CBHW071334130626
46556CB00004B/1897